THE MAKERS OF DARKNESS

D.R. Kane

CHAPTER ONE

In the fragile embrace of impending slumber, Jeff teetered on the edge of a hard-fought victory. His well-known adversary–the elusive grasp of sleep. Years of wrestling with this nocturnal enemy had created a familiar routine. A delicate dance to damper the restless anger that often accompanied his struggle to fall asleep.

As he slipped off to the soothing calmness, the elusive dreamlike state unfolded behind his closed eyelids. The gentle arms of sleep seemed to finally draw him into their comforting embrace. Just as the threshold of much-needed rest beckoned, a sudden, earth-shattering bang broke the tranquility. Jeff shot up in bed, his heart pounded and cold perspiration made his shirt cling uncomfortably to his body.

He was well acquainted with nightmares, but if the deafening bang he thought he heard was from a bad dream, why in the hell were his ears ringing? He was sure he had still been awake. Perhaps he was in the dream-like state of pure exhaustion that comes with insomnia.

Looking around his room, he saw, well...
nothing. It was Thanksgiving break and one of
the few benefits of being a high school teacher
was long holiday breaks and keeping your summer
vacation in perpetuity. So, in his usual ritual,
Jeff had drunk himself into a relative stupor and
stumbled to his bed sometime after midnight.
Despite the time reflected on his phone as he
picked it up from his bed stand, 1:13am, the
complete absence of light was unnerving.

Even this early in the morning he expected
to see some faint moonlight shining onto the floor
from his bedroom window or spot the orange glow
of the parking lot halogens in the distance. The
absolute darkness made his skin crawl. It was as
if someone had filled his room with black ink. He
tentatively held out his hand in front of his face
and could scarcely make out its silhouette. *Well,
I'm not blind, so that's good*, he thought.

Jeff lived in a half decent apartment complex
on the edge of the city and although it was
relatively clean and he didn't hear gunshots every
night, there were no overhead lights installed in
any of the rooms. A minor inconvenience for a
bachelor looking to avoid spending his pittance
of a teaching salary living in one of the more
happening areas of the city. The building had
four floors with 20 apartments to a floor, and a
small grassy area surrounded the 1970s era brick
building. It wasn't adorned with any of the more
appealing amenities that most other apartment

complexes were. There was no clubhouse, no gym, and the lobby wasn't equipped with a chic lounge. It was just an entrance leading to two elevators and a stairwell.

Jeff stretched out and grasped the small wheel of his bedside lamp and twisted it until he felt the snap.

When the light turned on, he stared at it, dumbfounded. The light, only two feet away from where he sat, illuminated his hand that was still attached to the control knob, and extended in a cone roughly four inches in diameter to the top of the bed stand. The bulb must be on its last leg, he thought, trying to reassure himself, but deeper within his consciousness he knew something was wrong.

As he picked his phone back up and tapped the flashlight icon, he noticed instead of bars showing signal strength, there were the small letters SOS.

Jeff slowly stood up as he activated his phone's flashlight and was thankful the ringing in his ears was subsiding. As he meandered over to his closet in search of a real flashlight, he heard a deep groan. He could only equate the sound to what he imagined an ocean liner's insides would make as its metal joints flexed against the unrelenting pressure of the sea. A chorus of chittering followed it up, interspersed with bird-like shrieks. Despite his lack of an ornithological degree, Jeff knew the shrieks were not coming from a bird that frequented the suburbs of Philadelphia.

With a quickened pace and mounting anxiety, Jeff swung open the door to his bedroom closet. Delving into the obscurity of the top shelf, he relied on touch, as his phone's flashlight struggled against the prevailing darkness. A cascade of miscellaneous items clattered to the floor before his fingers closed around the compact, metallic form of his flashlight.

A year prior, Jeff had acquired the flashlight, a purchase triggered by his early experiences working at high school football games. The gig predominantly involved shooing away cigarette-smoking teens lurking beneath the bleachers. Armed with a powerful device boasting over 5000 lumens, essentially a pocket-sized spotlight, Jeff thought it would have no problem piercing the pervasive darkness. However, when he summoned the light with a click, its powerful beam seemed hampered, barely extending three feet before succumbing to the voracious blackness. Adjusting the angle to illuminate his path, and avoid a potential face plant, Jeff navigated towards the window. The feeble glow of the flashlight struggled with the encroaching shadows.

A shiver made its way from the back of his head to the base of his spine as he observed the black wall staring back at him from the opposing side of the pane of glass. Just as he reassured himself that he had to be having another, albeit entirely new nightmare, a scream pierced its way through the neighboring apartment wall. A multitude of unintelligible shouts followed this, coming from distant rooms and a loud crash from the apartment above him. The report of gunfire sounded somewhere in the distance.

The noise of the pandemonium surrounding him faded out as the thump thump thump of his heartbeat drowned it out. His face was hot, and his legs suddenly felt like they were made of gelatin. Right as Jeff felt himself slipping off to the fuzzy sweet embrace of unconsciousness, a loud hammering came from his front door, along with a familiar voice shouting, "Help! Help! Please let me in, pleeeeaaase!" He was instantly snapped back to reality.

Jeff knew that voice, it was 3F. If he had had the courage to ask, he would have known her real name was Kara, but to Jeff the blue-eyed blond girl with the infectious smile across the hallway that he occasionally exchanged pleasantries with was just 3F. He hurriedly made his way to the door while illuminating the floor in front of him to navigate the minefield of his apartment. As Jeff fumbled with the chain lock, his mind raced, and he couldn't help but wonder how an average high school teacher, like himself, found himself at the epicenter of this nightmare.

His hands, slightly trembling, betrayed the calm facade he often wore. The darkness that enveloped his room seemed to mirror the shadows that occasionally crept into his thoughts during his long nights alone. Kara's familiar voice outside served as a stark reminder of the normalcy he craved in that moment, a respite from the relentless struggles that sometimes haunted him. He opened the door and Kara came rushing in, almost causing him to lose his balance and fall backwards. She quickly closed the door behind her.

CHAPTER TWO

Aberdeen Maryland

If you had asked the average Harford County, Maryland resident what the United States military and the massive number of civilian contractors did at Aberdeen proving grounds, their response would be simple. They test munitions. The weekly resounding booms coming from the military property would second this perception, however, the average Harford County, Maryland resident did not work at the base. For those individuals that were employed there, only a select few held the proper clearance to be privy to what was going on beneath the base.

Little did they know that an entrance obscured by a thick wall of ivy graced the rear of a nondescript building, simply labeled with black letters "utilities." This unassuming structure held something coveted by conspiracy theory scholars worldwide. In their defense, the United States government could not have accurately done a press release about the mystery being studied beneath the proving grounds. Even if they thought it wouldn't cause an all-out panic, they wouldn't know what to say. The fact was that they couldn't articulate exactly what it was beneath the proving grounds and any attempt to do so would be mere speculation. The government had, however, conscripted some of the best and brightest scientists in the world for the past several decades in an attempt to unwind the mystery.

Crystal scanned her badge, punched in her code, and waited for the audible click before pulling on the heavy steel entry door that led to the mantrap. She repeated the process within the mantrap, looking up at the camera mounted above the second door. As she descended the familiar dimly lit corridor, she reflected on the solitude she had grown accustomed to. Living alone wasn't just a consequence of her job; it was a conscious choice. Crystal found solace in the precision of her work, the controlled environment of the lab a stark contrast to the messy unpredictability of personal connections. She had tried the dating scene for a while but found most of the prospects to be dull or self-absorbed. Most people her age these days were more concerned with posting selfies to social media than making real, profound connections.

The lab, referred to as the labyrinth, below Aberdeen Proving Ground offered her a refuge from the imperfect world she often struggled to embrace.

The original civilian contractors working on the underground project were the ones to assign the lab its unofficial name. It wasn't that there were a series of passages to navigate or puzzles to solve to find your way to the dank underground warehouse– sized lab where Crystal and her colleagues worked. Its name had been passed down from the original group of scientists and military personnel who were assigned the frustrating task of attempting to decipher the giant slate colored orb that Crystal currently found herself staring at right in the core of the lab.

The lab had an ever-present smell of ozone, and the air was heavy with a feeling much like that of static electricity. She could never get used to the feeling of the fine brown hairs on her head and body standing as she entered the work area.

The orb was some sort of aerial craft. That much was clear when the United States Navy found it crashed on a small unnamed island 20 miles off the coast of Maryland in 1956. The various teams assigned to study the craft over the last 70 years had made little progress in unraveling the mysteries of the orb. There appeared to be no visible openings or seams on its smooth surface. No vents, windows, nor any sign of a way anyone or anything could access or exit the craft was present. They had conducted every test imaginable on the orb, they had tried X-rays, thermal imaging, neutron imaging and every other technology available to the powerhouse known as the United States government, all to no avail.

When attempting to see inside the craft

failed, they tried their hand at cracking the outside of the mysterious vehicle. Diamond coated blades shattered almost immediately after contacting its exterior, and explosives left little more than a dusty residue on the smooth surface of the anomaly. Concentrated lasers that would shear through titanium in an instant simply left a warm spot on the targeted area of the craft. The team had run out of ideas of late and found that their job consisted mostly of monitoring the orb while attempting to brainstorm new ideas.

A potentially monumental shift in the team's recent stagnation was the reason Crystal found herself returning to the base at nearly one in the morning. An array of video surveillance cameras that were watched by cleared defense contractors monitored the lab and its payload 24/7. The CDC's not only had the responsibility of securing the area surrounding the underground lab, but they were also given explicit instructions to promptly report any news up the chain of command. The chain of command would ultimately contact the researchers if anything unusual occurred during their absence.

Roughly 20 minutes ago, Crystal had received a call from one of the night monitor's supervisors. Apparently, there was an odd glow shining from the northern edge of the orb that they couldn't explain. She hurriedly threw on a shirt and a pair of faded blue jeans, took a half minute glance in the mirror to make a minuscule adjustment to her moused up bed head, grabbed her keys, and was on the road in under five minutes.

From where Crystal was currently standing at the base of the staircase, she could see a faint yellow glow coming from the opposite side of the orb. As she made her way around its base and approached the origin of the glow, she stared in amazement. Cut out of the previously smooth, unscathed surface of the orb was a five-foot tall by three feet wide opening. The yellow glow appeared to be emitting from the interior of the orb.

"Well I'll be damned," Crystal whispered to herself.

Decades before Crystal was briefed on the classified project, minds superior to hers informed her that there was, in fact, intelligent life outside the floating rock that the human race inhabited. The same group of researchers also concluded that these life forms were not located in any neighboring galaxy and even with a propulsion system far superior to anything mankind could fathom, that life form would have to live to around 50,000 years to reach earth alive.

That conclusion still held water, even with advances in human technology, so Crystal and her contemporary counterparts believed that whoever had sent this ship had either sent it unmanned or tapped into a way to alter time and space itself. This theory could also explain how the giant round orb looked like the complete antithesis of aerodynamics and managed to somehow crash from the sky.

Crystal knew that she should be donning one of the protective suits that the team wore when contacting the craft, more importantly she knew she should wait for the rest of the team to arrive before approaching the ship's mysterious gateway. Yet she tentatively reached out a hand toward the opening.

CHAPTER THREE

"Something was in my room! My window was cracked, it reached in, and-and my foot, I think whatever it was ate my toe, it ate my toe, Jeff!" Kara verbally vomited; her body wracked with sobs as she described the scene to Jeff through her tears. "When I woke up it was pitch dark and it felt like someone was grabbing my ankle. I thought some creep had broken in and was attacking me or something. I tried to kick free, turned on my phone's flashlight and saw something looking in the window next to my bed. It was horrible. It had gross, bulging eyes, two holes where its nose should be, and it was smiling with these oversized crooked teeth. I saw blood on its teeth and then it was slowly chewing something. When I looked down, I saw what looked like an extra-long, emaciated arm reaching in through the crack in my window and its hand was on my ankle."

Jeff glanced at the blood-soaked hand towel wrapped around Kara's foot as she continued.

"I kicked and twisted, and I couldn't break its grip until I took a nail file off my nightstand and stabbed the arm. I just kept stabbing it and it just kept chewing while staring at me with those giant eyes, like it didn't even faze it. Right when my arm was burning with exhaustion, it let go and vanished from the window. When I looked down, I noticed my little toe was missing and my bed was soaked in blood. I grabbed a hand towel and tied it around my foot to stop the bleeding and ran over here. Jeff, I, I, I cannot go back there."

Jeff stared at Kara in disbelief, ruminating on the horrifying tale she just recounted. "It was reaching in from your window on the third floor?"

"I know it sounds insane, but I am telling you that's what happened. I sure as hell didn't rip my toe off and almost smash down your door to come over and say hi," Kara responded.

"I'm not saying you're making it up. I'm just trying to make sense of what is going on here. These sounds coming from outside and all over the building, and some weird creature attacking you through your third-floor window, none of it makes any sense. I thought at first someone was playing an elaborate prank or there was a terrorist attack when I heard that giant explosion, but that doesn't explain this." Jeff slowly stepped back from Kara's flashlight. He had only stepped a few feet until the blackness blotted him out. It's like a black fog, or smoke from a tire burning pit with no smell, that can't be blown away." I feel like I'm either having the most vivid nightmare I've ever had, or someone slipped me some really strong hallucinogenic stuff."

"I would think the same thing in your position. But I'm telling you right now, I'm here, my foot is gushing real blood, and I'm scared out of my freaking mind. I don't know any more than you do about what is going on, but this isn't a damn dream," Kara said.

"We need to get that thing wrapped up in something better than a dish towel," Jeff said. He rifled through a drawer in his kitchen and pulled out a small first aid kit. Kara sat down on his kitchen floor and Jeff delicately removed the hand towel off her foot as she grimaced in pain. He began wrapping the bleeding stump where her toe once was and thought about her story. He continued, "I would say we could try the police, but my phone has no reception and if this extends any further than our apartment complex, I'm sure they've got bigger problems than us," Jeff explained.

"Yeah, mine's out too."

Just then, a low guttural roar tore through the air and the ground gently shook beneath their feet once, twice, then a third time. The two exchanged an anxious glance. Jeff could feel himself on the brink of hyperventilating as he attempted to process their situation. His head was pounding along with his heartbeat, and he felt sweat running down his back. He, again, felt like his legs were about to give out, but he knew he had to stay with it if they were going to survive.

"I don't think we should venture outside, if it's this dark everywhere we would be sitting ducks for whatever the hell is out there. We can try to stick it out here, but we have no idea how long this might last."

"Not going to argue with staying put, but we should try to fortify the windows or something. We could hole up here for a while if we need to. I've got a ton of food, I was planning on having my family over to see the new place for Thanksgiving next week and stocked up, but it's in my apartment." Kara whispered.

Jeff looked at Kara, his faded blue eyes reflecting a mix of concern and determination. "Look, if you're worried about your apartment, I can help you make sure it's safe. We can check it out and see if that thing is gone. If it's still there, we can always crash at my apartment for the time being."

"The thing took off after you put a bunch of holes in its arm though, so it's hopefully long gone by now," he said, but his face did not match the certainty of his tone.

Kara's voice trembled as she confessed, "I was in a total panic when I ran out; I didn't have a chance to shut the window. What's stopping it, or whatever else we're hearing out there from coming in?"

Jeff pondered their predicament, gesturing

toward the ominous darkness outside his window. "Our two options are to hunker down here or try to wander out into this. We have no idea how long this could go on. Regardless of what we decide, we should be prepared. I'm sure you'll want shoes," he added, nodding towards Kara's bare feet. "And we should grab some backpacks to stock up on essentials, just in case we need to leave quickly."

"Do you have anything we can use to defend ourselves in here?" Kara asked, her eyes scanning the room for potential weapons.

Jeff contemplated for a moment. "An old baseball bat and some kitchen knives are the best I can do."

Kara sighed, "I was hoping for a gun, but better than nothing, I guess. I really don't want to go back there." The tension in the room grew as the reality of their situation sank in. They were under attack, but by what? The unnatural sounds coming through the walls did little to clarify the situation.

Jeff and Kara cautiously entered the hallway, their flashlights scarcely cutting through the suffocating darkness that seemed to envelop them like black water. The beams revealed a gruesome trail of blood on the floor, a sinister testament to the horrors that were unfolding around them. Distant screams mingled with eerie non-human shrieks, created an unhinged symphony echoing through the apartment complex and beyond.

Their every step was accompanied by the

unsettling squelch of something beneath their feet. As they moved forward, the air grew colder, and the oppressive atmosphere seemed to close in around them. Shadows danced on the walls, playing tricks on their senses.

Reaching Kara's apartment, they hesitated before entering. The door creaked open, revealing an uncanny stillness. Everything appeared undisturbed, as if the apartment had escaped the clutches of whatever nightmare was plaguing the world. A collective breath of relief floated in the air as their flashlights swept across familiar furniture and belongings.

Their reprieve was short-lived. As they stepped further into the apartment, a subtle noise echoed—an unnerving whisper or a distant shuffle. The air, once tinged with relief, now held a quiet tension. Shadows seemed to elongate, casting doubt on the safety they hoped they'd found.

"It was probably from outside," Jeff whispered, attempting to calm both Kara and himself.

Kara exchanged a nervous glance with Jeff. "I'm sorry, I'm not staying here. I don't feel safe. Let's just grab what we can and get out." She quickly picked up a pair of sneakers near the front door.

Understanding the urgency in Kara's voice, Jeff nodded in agreement. They both knew the importance of being prepared, especially given the mysterious circumstances they found themselves in. They headed to the kitchen, aware that even in the apparent calm, something insidious could be lurking just beyond the reach of their feeble beams of light. The unknown horrors that awaited them remained concealed, heightening the suspense within the confines of Kara's apartment.

With a sense of urgency, they filled the backpacks they had brought from Jeff's apartment with food and supplies from Kara's kitchen. Every sound seemed amplified as they moved, the tension palpable in the air. Just as they secured the last of the supplies, an unexpected draft caught their attention, drawing their gaze to the now fully opened window.

Kara, her eyes wide with alarm, pointed out the anomaly. "That window wasn't fully open when we came in." Her voice trembled slightly, reigniting the unease over their situation and reinforcing their decision to leave as quickly as possible.

Suddenly, a grotesque figure materialized, emerging from the shadows. It bore a semblance to humanity but deviated in nightmarish ways —a living caricature, larger than any human, with a colossal head and disproportionately large, misshapen eyes. Its mouth, stained with crimson hues, revealed oversized and irregularly placed teeth. The arm, previously wounded by Kara's blade, now oozed a dark, inky substance. Oddly out of place, the creature was wearing a gore smeared white bathrobe.

Twisted limbs moved awkwardly beneath it, and a chilling smile played on its disturbing human-like face. The creature's presence, marked by the grotesque fusion of familiar and otherworldly features, sent an icy chill through Jeff as he realized Kara's story had not been exaggerated. As the monstrosity slowly closed the distance, Jeff put himself between Kara and it, raising his baseball bat.

CHAPTER FOUR

Philadelphia Pennsylvania

Ken stared out the windshield of his cruiser observing the abundant foot traffic that was commonplace for this part of the city even at the current time of 2:30am. Ken's grizzled exterior bore witness to the physical toll of the job, his body a testament to the countless struggles he had faced and overcome. He felt the weight of his years in law enforcement, a weariness that transcended the physical, etched into the lines of his hardened expression.

He observed the usual stumbling of the unfortunate souls here to get their fix. Their impromptu pharmacists side eyed Ken as they walked by his cruiser. They were all sure to give a wide berth out of respect for the black furred, wild-eyed maniac peering at them through the grates of the back window and emitting a low growl.

It wasn't anything personal for Loki, Ken's K9. He just didn't prefer anyone getting close to his car. Ken reached back through the porthole in between the seats and made a smooching sound to summon Loki away from the window and felt Loki's reassuring warm tongue on his hand.

"It's okay they aren't bothering you, who's my good man?" Ken asked gently.

The thump thump thump of Loki's tail on the rear door started slowly and then crescendoed to a jackhammer when Ken said, "Should... we... get a walk?"

There was a time not too long ago that Ken would have been out of his car and hiding in the alley waiting to observe the supplier exchanging their products for cash. He'd pop out, chase them down, and fight them into cuffs. Back then, he thought that their short time in city jail would make them reconsider their ways. A combination of locking up the same repeat offenders dozens of times, a gunshot wound, and a myriad of other injuries, Ken had long ago resigned from proactive enforcement.

Years on the job had left Ken jaded. His faith in humankind was nearly nonexistent, and he tended to expect the worst from people. Growing up in poverty and seeing the struggles of the lower half had made him want to become a cop to help others. The frequent traumas and assaults, both physical and verbal, had trained him to believe that people did not appreciate his need to help. He could still fire into action to save a gunshot victim or stop an assault in progress, but he had shifted more to the ounce of prevention mindset, even though he wasn't sure there was a cure. That's why he found himself here, in one of the busiest open-air drug markets in the city at this time of night. He hoped to deter another shooting or homicide for at least the next couple of hours. He was on overtime and in a couple hours he'd be off for three whole days.

Ken drove a few blocks to a stretch of road that led to a heavily wooded park to take Loki out for a stroll. As he opened the back door and deftly caught the collar of the fur rocket that blasted out while attaching his leash, he scanned the dimly lit surroundings with a hint of caution. Ken muttered to himself, "please don't find a body on this walk buddy." His brown hair, speckled with strands of gray, gave him a distinguished appearance. Despite being in his forties and the sometimes-sedentary nature of patrolling in a vehicle most of his working life, Ken remained relatively fit. He had gotten a little softer in the mid-section, but he still retained most of the muscle that years of working out had built.

Ken had just loaded Loki back into his car and shut the door when the Malinois growled. Ken looked around and, seeing that there was no one around, said, "You must be seeing stuff buddy. There isn't a soul around." His eyes flicked to Loki's, noting the intensity of the dog's gaze reflected in his own green eyes. He got into the vehicle and tried to summon the pooch to poke his head through the seats again, but saw that Loki was still staring out the driver's side rear door growling, his hackles standing stiffly.

What has gotten into him? Ken thought to himself as he drove back to the post he had been overseeing. Upon returning to the corner he had been posted at, Ken pulled up to the curb and put his cruiser into park. He was just settling back into watching the hustle of the street when suddenly, an ear-shattering boom cut through the quiet night, causing Ken to nearly jump out of his seat. Loki, overcome with a frenzy of barks, confirmed the disturbance. Through the windshield, Ken realized the world had plunged into darkness, a disquieting and blinding void that entrenched his surroundings.

Ken's practiced hand moved swiftly to activate the spotlight, a narrow beam that cut through the oppressive darkness, revealing only a limited radius of about five feet. In this newfound illumination, the contours of the city took on a ghostly quality, casting long shadows that seemed to dance with malevolence. Amid the haunting visual display, an unsettling chorus of sounds punctuated the night: distant screams echoed through the desolate streets, the desperate pleas of others caught in the same malevolent dance.

The spotlight revealed the twisted shapes of buildings and alleys. When he cracked his window it exposed unnatural sounds, guttural growls, chittering and grinding noises. The cityscape transformed into a horrific circus, where the interplay of light and darkness made Ken wish he was currently anywhere else.

As the light pierced the veil of obscurity, an unexpected scene unfolded. A drug dealer, once an adversary of Ken, stumbled into view, his gaunt and bloodied form limping through the dimly lit abyss. Still clutched in his barely attached right hand dangled a pistol. His anguished screams for help echoed through the desolate streets, adding to the symphony of misery surrounding Ken.

Desperation etched across his face, the struggling man sprinted towards Ken's cruiser, his salvation seemingly within reach. Yet at the precise moment he neared the haven of the passenger door, a monstrous hand nearly the size of Ken's vehicle emerged from the shadows. Misshapen and equipped with malformed, cracked black nails, the appendage plunged into the beam of the spotlight, seizing the terrified figure.

Just as the man disappeared from the circle of light, his screams halted, replaced by a gut-wrenching crunch reverberating through the night air. A gory feast transpired in the shroud of darkness.

A jolt of primal fear surged through Ken, transforming his veins into icy rivers as the once-familiar city unraveled into a phantasmagoria of terror. The contours of the slivers of the urban landscape that Ken could see when directing his spotlight twisted into grotesque shapes that loomed threateningly.

The dissonant chorus of distant screams

clawed at Ken's senses, filling the air with a haunting melody of despair. His breath quickened, each inhalation saturated with the acrid taste of fear, as if the very air conspired against him.

After breaking free from his paralysis, Ken discerned an unusual stillness in the typically incessant police radio chatter. Fingers tense, he pressed the mic button and uttered," 'K912 here. Anyone there?" The hush that followed conveyed not just a blackout but also a disruption of the department's radio signals. Glancing at his phone, which displayed zero bars, Ken realized the phone towers were out too.

As the vision of the monstrous hand replayed in his head, his mind turned to Sarah, waiting at home with their toddler, Grant. *If this shit extends beyond the city*, he thought, *I need to get home right now*. With this, Ken aimed his spotlight on where he judged the center of the road to be and began slowly speeding up. "We gotta get home to mommy and the boy," he said to Loki.

With a 45-minute drive on the best of days, Ken now faced an extended trek. Limited visibility, only a handful of feet in front of his vehicle, hinted at a considerably longer journey home to his family.

The carnage was clear from the moment they started moving. He constantly had to zigzag around abandoned cars within the roadway. His spotlight scanned a stalled sedan stopped diagonally across the lane. He saw the windshield had a hole the size of a bowling bowl in it that was rimmed with blood and an errant chunk of hair. Ken's skin crawled as the human shrieks interspersed with ghostly moaning sounds escalated.

As Ken continued his expedition, the spotlight caught a chilling sight–a colossal stalk-like leg descended from the shadows, mercilessly crushing a car within the beam's narrow focus. The leg then ascended into the blackness beyond the reach of his spotlight with the vehicle still attached to it. Glass tinkled down on his cruiser like sleet raining down from the darkness above.

Further down the road, the spotlight revealed a telephone pole with an enormous, otherworldly nest that resembled a wasp's hive. The buzzing and fluttering wings of gigantic creatures filled the air. Ken couldn't look away as the spotlight illuminated one creature carrying a screaming man towards the nest, where others eagerly awaited. The man's body had grotesque swellings the size of softballs, oozing a yellow liquid. The man feebly battered at the body of the creature as he and the flying monster disappeared inside an opening of the nest, the rest of the creatures followed into the opening for a horrific feast.

Tension gripped him as he processed the bizarre and distressing scene. The spotlight, once a tool of his trade in the city, now exposed the twisted realities that lay hidden in the darkness outside. Determined, Ken pressed on, the road home became a surreal journey fraught with unknown terrors. The safety of his family remained the driving force propelling him through the haunting night.

Ken's precinct sat on the outskirts of the city, a desolate outpost marking the beginning of the now perilous journey he had to undertake to reach home. The ambient glow of his spotlight led him through the foreboding darkness as he maneuvered into the precinct's back lot. Relief initially embraced him when the first police cruiser appeared untouched. However, tranquility swiftly slipped away as his spotlight landed on the next parking spot, labeled "shift commander." Instead of the familiar sight of the shift commander's SUV, he was confronted with a disturbing cocoon-like structure. The grotesque mass loomed from within the darkness. Red and blue lights protruded mysteriously from the top, the only sign that the SUV lay concealed within the startling chrysalis.

Ken directed the beam of light towards the thick steel door, the rear entrance of the building, and a shiver ran through him as his eyes traced the four deeply carved gashes running down its center. It was the first time Ken genuinely appreciated the windowless, fortress-like precinct where he had spent the past 14 years. Despite the desire to check on his partners and replenish his ammunition, the haunting scenes along his brief journey gave him pause. He met the idea of making a dash for the door with hesitation; there was no way he would leave his partner alone in the car amidst the chaos.

Loki, who had since ceased growling, remained on high alert in the back of the vehicle. Pacing back and forth, he panted heavily, desensitized by the relentless calamity around them. The dog eyed him questioningly as they came to a stop in the familiar lot of the station house. The slight orange glow at the corner of the building informed him that either the power was on or the unreliable generator had actually worked this time.

"Hey boy, you think we can make it inside there?" Ken inquired of the Malinois.

Loki's tail waved in anticipation, a silent yet affirmative response to Ken's question.

Ken pressed the under-dash button, releasing the Mossberg 12-gauge shotgun from the passenger side of the vehicle. Gripping the gun, he activated the attached light, illuminating a meager path in the black air. Glancing over his shoulder, he commanded, "With me, boy." Loki affirmed with an excited whine, understanding that he was to stay by his handler's side.

Ken took a moment, bracing himself for the impending sprint to the steel door. As he readied himself, he pondered, How long did it normally take him to punch in his code on the Hersch pad that unlocked the back door? Two seconds, maybe... He hoped to hell that it was quick enough. The urgency of the situation loomed overhead, and Ken felt the ticking of each passing second as he wrestled with what he was about to do.

With adrenaline coursing through his veins, Ken sprinted towards the looming steel door. Fumbling with his keys, he urgently popped open the dog door of his cruiser. Loki, a blur of fur beside him, joined in the mad dash, their feet pounding against the pavement in a desperate rhythm. In the ominous night sky, a shrieking blur, part flying horror, part deformed human, arced overhead. Its grotesque form took a menacing swipe at Ken, a reminder of the nightmarish chaos surrounding them.

The rush of wind and the creature's unearthly silhouette fueled Ken's urgency. As they closed in on the door, Ken began punching in his access code on the security pad, each digit feeling like an eternity. The ground behind him rustled with a skittering sound, as if something sensing their movements had begun to pursue them. The urgency of unlocking the door intensified, and Ken felt the weight of the unknown closing in with each digit he entered, a race against time which Ken sensed he may run out of. His loyal companion stood butt to butt with Ken, leaping and furiously snapping at the unseen horrors.

CHAPTER FIVE

A distant memory materialized into Crystal's brain. It played inside her head as if shown within the opening of the craft from a projector. She saw herself in a brightly lit room at the University of Maryland filled with her peers giving a presentation on the interdimensional hypothesis. She remembered feeling attacked and belittled by the professor sitting in the front row as he ridiculed the absurdity of the theory of multiple planes of existence explaining the sightings of UFOs. Muffled shouting pierced its way into her waking dream and an electric charge coursed through her body as she retracted her hand from the doorway and returned to the present.

"Crystal, what the hell are you doing? Get away from there!" Patrick's urgent voice cut through the disorienting soundscape. It snapped her back to the present, but the lingering remnants of the unsettling memory clung to her consciousness like a ghostly residue, leaving her shaken and questioning the blurred boundaries between her past and the enigmatic portal before her.

As Patrick approached the frozen scene, his tall and lean frame moved with a sense of urgency. The dim glow from the lab's overhead lights revealed the lines of fatigue traced on his face, evidence of countless nights spent immersed in the mysteries of their shared project. His salt-and-pepper hair, usually meticulously combed, now stood in disarray, reflecting the chaos of the situation before him. Despite the weariness, determination burned in his eyes, a testament to the unwavering commitment he held to the mysterious project that had bound him to Crystal for years.

Unlike Crystal, Patrick had a family back home, and that was the sole reason he wasn't the first of the researchers to make it to the lab after the call went out. Waking up in the early morning became more challenging, with two young children at home. Patrick was still the most dedicated member of the team; his other responsibilities just meant he was spread thin these days.

As Crystal stood there, haunted by the echoes of that university confrontation, she met Patrick's intense gaze. The weight of his dedication mirrored the gravity of the mysteries they unraveled together. His words lingered in the charged air, urging her away from the pulsating gateway. She could not find the words to explain what had happened when she had touched the opening.

In the dim lab, the orb's glow intensified, casting shadows that danced across the walls. Crystal couldn't get rid of the impression that the interdimensional hypothesis, once ridiculed, was unfolding in a manner that was beyond understanding. The intersection of her past and the present mystery blurred further, creating a vertigo-like feeling.

Patrick's voice broke through her thoughts. "We need to assess this situation carefully, Crystal. This could be the breakthrough we've been looking for, but it could also be very dangerous. We don't know what this thing is capable of."

A humming coming from the orb that Crystal had just now registered intensified, resonating with the uncertainty in the room. Crystal hesitated, torn between the allure of discovery and the safety of the lab outside of the ship. It felt as if the craft was enticing her to walk inside and see all the wonders. She and many others had worked so many years to figure out.

Patrick's hand on her shoulder managed to ground her. "Crystal, are you with me? I think you need to back away now."

"Yeah," she mumbled as she slowly turned, allowing Patrick's reassuring grip to guide her while fighting the urge to break free and rush back into the glow of the opening. By the time Crystal was standing back on the landing that oversaw the craft, the other researchers were making their way down the staircase to join her and Patrick.

"What's up with you two, and what did you do to the monitoring system?" Mindy asked. Mindy, a seasoned researcher with an air of intellectual authority, had developed a deep-seated curiosity over her time with the team. Her short-cropped hair and glasses gave her a distinctive appearance that was often matched by her insightful observations.

Patrick, visibly distraught, responded, "I honestly don't know, but don't go near that fucking thing without a suit on," as he pointed towards the orb, "It has a strange pull to it. I found Crystal in a daze, about to walk into the opening, and when I got close to help her, I could feel it. Mindy, Scott work on getting the monitoring systems back up, and everyone get your suits on!"

The researchers hurriedly donned their suits, the metallic clang of zippers and hushed whispers amplifying the tense atmosphere. Crystal's gaze remained fixated on the dormant monitors, the void on the screens mirrored the bewilderment now clear on her face.

Mindy, adjusting her suit with a hint of skepticism, questioned, "What's so dangerous about that thing, Patrick? It's been dormant for half a century, how much power can really be stored up in it?"

Patrick's eyes betrayed a mixture of fear and fascination. "I cannot explain it, but it's like it wants us to go into the doorway. Crystal was ready to step inside, and I felt something pulling at me too."

The crew, now suited up, exchanged uneasy glances when they neared the dormant control center. Scott furrowed his brow, fingers dancing across the keyboard, attempting to revive the silent screens that once pulsated with vital data. As the first monitor flickered to life, a collective sigh of relief swept through the group.

Mindy's eyes darted between the screens and the mysterious orb. "Whatever's happening, we need to document it."

Patrick, his demeanor resolute, agreed. "Yeah, but we should really keep our distance as much as possible. This isn't like anything we've encountered before."

The orb's hum resonated once more, a sinister melody that seemed to echo through the chamber. As the researchers tentatively approached, the air became charged with an electrical energy that they could feel, a sense that the fabric of their reality hung by a thread.

As the remaining monitors flickered back to life, casting an eerie glow on the tense faces of the research team, Scott's eyes widened in disbelief. He frantically pointed to the readings, his voice laden with urgency, "Crystal, look at this! The energy levels are off the charts." Crystal's eyes widened, mirroring the collective astonishment of the group. The once-silent screens now danced with erratic waves of energy, a pulsating force that seemed to defy the laws of physics.

Mindy, adjusting the collar of her suit, added with a hint of concern, "And check out the radiation levels. They're spiking dangerously high. Good thing we're suited up," Mindy said, her gloved hand instinctively patting the protective layers.

The team exchanged uneasy glances, the gravity of the situation sinking in. Patrick, ever vigilant, surveyed the monitors and the menacingly vibrant orb. "We need to find out what triggered this sudden surge. This craft has been dormant for over 60 years. It shouldn't be emitting this kind of energy."

"We're going to have to go inside. If there was a way to deactivate this thing from the outside, we would've found it by now," Crystal shouted over the humming.

Mindy's apprehension cut through the tense air. "How can we be certain there's a way to deactivate it inside? No one was here to activate it in the first place. I, for one, don't fancy stepping into that thing."

Patrick surveyed the room, his expression a mix of determination and caution. "We need to exhaust all our options before taking that step, but if going inside is our only recourse, I'll go."

Crystal, undeterred by the risk, met Patrick's gaze. "If it comes down to that, count me in. We can't let it keep running. Who knows what it will do?" The resolute agreement hung in the air, sealing their collective resolve to confront the mysteries that lay within the once dormant vessel.

The monitors' frantic beeping reverberated through the tense atmosphere, drowning out the ominous hum emanating from the orb. The crew exchanged alarmed glances as the readings spiraled into the danger zone, a silent warning of the escalating danger of the situation.

Scott, fingers again flying across the keyboard, his mop top hair in shambles, desperately tried to decipher where the escalating energy levels were coming from. Beads of sweat formed on his forehead as he muttered, "There's nothing I can do from here. This wasn't an expected contingency. These are monitoring systems. I've got no way of controlling anything."

Crystal, appearing calm amidst the calamity, said, "Don't we have access to exploratory drones? We could try to send them in and see what we can see. It beats risking our hides."

Patrick, squinting in concentration, replied, "Yeah, the base has bomb robots, and we could definitely get our hands on one. Let me make a call."

Ten minutes later, the team mobilized to deploy the bomb robot. The humming from the orb reached a fever pitch. The air in the lab crackled with a palpable tension, heightening the awareness that they were on the precipice of uncovering something beyond their understanding.

The bomb robot, a sophisticated piece of technology, looked indestructible with its sturdy, angular frame. Gleaming metal and matte black surfaces covered its robust exterior. The machine housed a myriad of sensors and cameras for precise maneuvering. Its articulated limbs moved with a mechanical grace; each joint a testament to engineering precision. A central control panel displayed a menagerie of buttons and screens, allowing skilled operators to navigate high-stakes situations from a safe distance.

Crystal couldn't dismiss the feeling that the craft held secrets that transcended the boundaries of conventional science. The half century old mysteries, adding to the enigma that gripped the research team.

Patrick surveyed the lab, his gaze meeting Crystal's. "Stay alert. We're navigating uncharted territory here. There's no saying what we might find in there, and we need to be prepared for whatever this thing has in store."

As Crystal piloted the vehicle into the glowing gateway, the monitors displayed a surreal tableau of energy fluctuations. The crew, standing on the threshold of the unknown, braced themselves for the revelations that awaited them within the once dormant vessel.

CHAPTER SIX

The beep of the final digit Ken punched into the access pad echoed through his mind, yet it could not drown out the symphony of terror playing behind him. The skittering sounds moved ever closer mixing with the frantic barking of Loki. These sounds were accompanied by a sharp snapping that indicated whatever was closing in on him was too close to Loki. Ken turned the handle of the door and pulled it open while simultaneously looking over his shoulder for his companion.

His heart, already in his throat, shuddered for a moment when he didn't spot the k9. Every electrical firing within the fibers of the lizard part of his brain was screaming to shut the heavy steel door, put the door between him and the carnival of horrors that were tight on his heels. But Loki was part of his family, and he would not leave the dog. He raised the shotgun, its light scantily piercing the darkness, and stepped away from the door. The promise of the safety of the steel door began to close behind him. Out of nowhere, Loki rocketed into the diminishing opening and Ken caught the door before it could shut him out.

As Ken pulled the door closed behind him, pressing his weight against it, he looked at his dog with astonishment. The Malinois looked back at him, tail wagging as he released his clenched jaws, dropping what first appeared to be a human arm at Ken's feet. The dog happily waited for Ken to pick it up, as if he had just retrieved a stick for his master. Further inspection with Ken's flashlight revealed that the limb was grotesquely deformed, a mockery of an actual human arm. It was twice the length of even the largest man's arm and emaciated; the flesh slid off the black bone with a touch of Ken's boot.

"What in the hell is going on here boy?" Ken whispered to the elated pooch.

Ken raised the flashlight to the hallway in front of them as he stepped over the discarded limb. He abruptly stopped after a few quick steps when the flashlight illuminated a wall of chairs, tables, and police shields that were stacked to the ceiling.

"Hey, anyone here? It's Ken," he shouted.

A rustling sound from beyond the fortification made Loki let out a low, vibrating growl. Ken took a step back and raised the shotgun, ready for whatever additional monstrosities the night was prepared to throw at him. He was already tired of running. Loki's gory present to Ken proved that the beasts could be harmed. He didn't like his chances with some of the behemoths he had witnessed outside, but within the confines of the station house, he was much more confident. He surmised that the twelve gauge and its double zero buckshot contained within a magnum shell was enough to drop anything that could fit within the walls of the station. That was if Ken could fire a shot before a creature closed in within the blinding darkness.

For this he trusted in his partner, Loki's nose was not only good at locating narcotics, but sensitive to organic matter. Ken knew the dog could smell a hidden criminal in the night in the middle of the woods, and he presumed the carnival of horrors he had witnessed in his journey thus far were not scentless. So, he trusted his partner's growl and was ready to respond to whatever was creeping toward them beyond the barricade.

Then, from across the barrier, a dim light shined through the cracks. "Ken, is that you?"

"Mark? Shit man, I am glad to hear your voice. What the hell is going on? How are you holding up, and where the hell is everyone?" Ken responded.

Mark, a formidable veteran officer who long ago could have retired, was a familiar and well-liked member of the precinct. He stood at a whopping 6'5 and dwarfed Ken. The big man had kept working for a sense of purpose and spent most of his time in the station fielding calls from citizens and assigning them to the proper units. He parted the police shield doorway within the barricade and urged Ken inside with a quick wave of his hand.

"Get on this side of the barricade man. I don't think many of them made it in, but the ones that did are on that side of the station. We can talk when you're over here."

Ken promptly obliged, Loki slinking in front of him to jump up and give the familiar large man a lick on the hand.

Ken watched the Malinois. "Looks like he's as happy to see you as I am, where's the cavalry?"

Mark's weary face appeared through the shadows as he slid the shield back into the barricade slot. "Glad you made it, Ken. The situation's gone to shit. We've lost contact with most of the units, and those things..." He hesitated, glancing nervously toward the barricaded entrance. "They're not human. I, I don't know what they are. It's like a living nightmare out there."

Ken's gaze sharpened, his senses on high alert. "What are they Mark? Have you seen any of them up close?"

Mark shook his head, a haunted expression in his eyes. "Not clearly, but enough to know we're dealing with something beyond anything we've been trained on. We've got a few survivors holed up here, and we need a plan. The cavalry, as you put it, isn't coming. We're on our own."

Ken remained silent, absorbing the implications of what Mark had just told him. If the entire precinct wasn't present and planning a response, the situation was more dire than he thought.

Mark's voice dropped to a hushed tone, barely audible over the terrifying sounds beyond the barricade. "When that loud ass bang rang out, turning off the stars, the world outside transformed. Inhuman sounds filled the air, and our police radios went silent, just like the phones. We had no choice but to send a team out to assess the situation, promising to check in every 30 minutes in person."

He paused, the weight of the unspoken hanging heavily in the air. "It's been hours Ken. Only one of the seven who ventured out returned, and he was... he was a wreck. Battered, bloody, and mute. Whatever is out there, it's tearing through everything we know, and it's inside that black fog."

Mark's eyes held a shaken look as he continued, "The survivors here are a handful of officers who were doing administrative work–paperwork and such. They were not part of the reconnaissance group. We've also got a few citizens from the city who made it here shortly after the shit hit the fan." Mark shifted uncomfortably. "One local, an older man, told me how he ended up here. He was walking his dog, a golden retriever, when it happened. The darkness descended, and he said he heard this unexplainable shriek. Something yanked the leash hard, sending him sprawling on his face. When he recovered, the dog was gone, and all that remained was a clump of bloody fur where the collar snapped."

Mark's jaw clenched, his voice tense. "Then, as he struggled to his feet, a gigantic foot, a giant fucking foot Ken, slammed down beside him. He ran for his life, all the while hearing unexplainable sounds and feeling the ground rumble. At first, I thought the guy was nuts. I was about to start the paperwork to have him admitted to the hospital, but then the second guy that showed up, I got a glimpse...

"Gary and I opened the back door where this guy was banging, shouting for his life. We already knew something was going on, so we opened up and then...as the guy stumbled through the door. We tried to figure out what he was screaming about. The guy was so freaked out we couldn't understand him. Gary was holding the door and something, like a twisted fucking monster attacked him. I only caught a glimpse, but from what I thought I saw, an oversized head with horns, yellow skin, and the blackest eyes–it defied the laws of nature. I'll never forget those black eyes."

"It bit Gary's hand clean off and pulled him into the darkness outside. The guy who had rushed in knocked me over, and the other survivors in here dragged me back. We put together this barrier you see to try to keep them on that side of the building.

"The shapes in the blackness were hard to see, but before the door shut, a few blurs rushed in through the opening. So, something is in here on the other half of the station. Nothing has tried the barrier yet, but we've been hearing something moving around and making a groaning sound over there."

Ken nodded his head in understanding. "On any other night I would call the white suits to throw you in a padded room, but the stuff I've seen on my way here…Ken paused before finishing, "It's not explainable, it's like hell on earth."

In the dimly lit, barricaded hallway, Mark and Ken, both seasoned officers, exchanged glances that spoke volumes of shared experiences and unspoken camaraderie. The muffled sounds of distant chaos echoed through the walls of the police station, emphasizing the urgency of their situation.

"Ken," Mark began, his voice firm but laced with concern. "We can't leave these things inside. Whatever they are, this barricade will not hold them forever, and the survivors in the roll call room need us. We have to clear the other half of the station."

Ken, gripping his weapon tighter, nodded in agreement. "I get it, Mark, but I can't be here for long. My family is back home, and I need to make sure they're safe. Depending on how far this goes, I've got one hell of a drive to get there."

Mark, understanding the gravity of Ken's

words, spoke with determination. "I won't ask you to stay longer than it takes us to clear this place. If we can secure the other half of the station, I'll get you supplied and help find a way for you to get home. We can't leave them in here."

Ken hesitated, then nodded in reluctant agreement. "Alright, Mark. I'll help you clear the station, but we need to move fast. Once it's secure, I'm heading home to my family."

Grateful for Ken's support, Mark clapped a hand on his shoulder. "Thank you Ken. Let's do this together, and I promise we'll find a way to help get you home safely."

With a shared nod, Mark and Ken readied themselves to face the unknown horrors lurking in the station's hallways.

Ken looked at Loki. "Search boy, but stay close." Loki, tail wagging, walked and sat in front of the impromptu doorway of the barricade, eager to get to work.

CHAPTER SEVEN

Jeff was averagely built for a guy in his mid-thirties. He played sports in high school, but high school was a long time ago. Right now, at his spot in between the monstrosity and Kara, a baseball bat overhead, he was both terrified yet determined. The creature reached out for Jeff with one long, deformed limb while making a low moaning sound. Jeff took a half step back and brought the bat down with every ounce of strength he had and felt a comforting thump, confirming he had hit his target. The abomination withdrew its arm, made a loud screeching noise, and retreated a few feet back.

Seeing the momentary opening, Jeff yelled, "Run!"

He spun on his heels and sprinted for the front door of Kara's apartment. As the pair made their way through the kitchen, the scrambling sounds of frantic claws on the linoleum floor informed them that another pursuer had just made it to the kitchen. Jeff's heart was pounding uncontrollably, his breathing was near hyperventilating as they threw open the apartment door and made it to Jeff's door. Jeff fumbled with the keys in the near darkness, finally finding the right one. He frantically rushed to insert the key in its slot.

Kara shouted, "Hurry, they're right behind us!"

Jeff could hear the door to Kara's apartment slam open, hitting the wall and the padding on the hallway floor as the pursuing creatures closed in. With trembling hands, Jeff managed to insert the key, turning it just in time to swing the door open. He and Kara stumbled into the safety of Jeff's apartment, breathless and terrified.

As the door slammed shut behind them, a heavy silence settled, broken only by the muffled sounds of the monsters lingering outside. Jeff, still gripping the baseball bat, exchanged a glance with Kara, both acknowledging the reality of the situation. Shadows danced eerily on the walls as they caught their breath in the dimly lit room.

Suddenly, a low growl echoed through the hallway, sending shivers down their spines. Something started scratching at the door with desperate claws, seeking entry. Jeff knew they needed a plan, a way to survive the night that seemed increasingly suffocating.

Kara, wide-eyed and trembling, asked, "What do we do now?"

Jeff panting heavily responded, "We have to reinforce this door so these things don't find their way in, and it would probably be a good idea to put something in front of the windows too. Here, help me with this," he said gripping the side of a bookcase next to the entryway. It was an ancient, sturdily built piece he had picked up for a bargain at a secondhand shop. The pair slid the heavy case in place, blocking the door as it thumped from another exterior blow.

In a rush, Jeff hurried to his entryway closet, frantically sifting through its contents until he unearthed a small cordless drill with screws and a pair of corn hole tables. "This will have to work for the windows; I don't have any spare wood lying around," he muttered out loud. Striding into the living room, he positioned one table against the window and began the precarious task of securing it. The dim light flickered. Jeff worked feverishly to fortify his fragile sanctuary. Yet, an unsettling feeling lingered, as if an unseen presence observed his every move, shrouding the room in an atmosphere of dread.

Amid the unrelenting terror, Jeff felt another emotion he hadn't felt in quite some time: purpose. Despite the dire circumstance he and Kara currently found themselves in, Jeff had found that the mundaneness of the last few years of his life had steadily beaten him into a profound depression. He had a secure job, still living parents that loved him, yet an unshakable emptiness lingered. His once vibrant blue eyes now mirrored the desolation within, framed by deepening lines drawn on his face by the weight of an invisible burden. The walls of his soul seemed to echo with the haunting whispers of his own discontent, a disquiet that manifested itself in drinking too much and sleeping too little. Even in the dim light of their predicament, one could sense a subtle, desolate aura that clung to him, as if shadows from a realm beyond were drawn to the void within him.

Jeff had made feeble attempts at trying all the self-help recommendations for dealing with depression. He still went for runs a few times a week, made a halfhearted attempt at eating healthy and kept a social life. He even tried seeing a therapist for a few months, but after several sessions, he felt his problems were not important enough to take up the time of a professional. However, tonight, faced with inexplicable horror, he felt a glimmer of the drive he once held for life.

As he made his way to the second window of the apartment in his bedroom, he asked Kara, "Can you hold the light on this for me?"

"How long have you lived here?" Kara asked as she followed him into the room with the light.

Kara had known Jeff since she had moved in a year ago, but had only spoken to him in brief exchanges. He seemed like a shy guy and often responded to her hellos before quickly averting his eyes from hers.

This was her second apartment since graduating college, but the first one that wasn't near her family on the opposite side of the state in Pittsburgh. She missed being close to her family and the atmosphere of the steel city, but social worker jobs near Philadelphia paid better. And the student loans she had been carrying for almost a decade now were not going to pay themselves. On several occasions she had thought of asking Jeff out for a drink. He seemed like a genuinely nice person, although he carried a morose look in his eyes that she was curious about.

After moving to Philadelphia, she had made a few coworker friends, but they rarely got together outside of work. The mental drain of trying to help people in some of the hardest times of their life was not something you wanted to continue thinking about over drinks when you left work. She had been struggling lately with empathy fatigue, a strange side effect of spending all day hurting for other's predicaments that somehow dulled the emotion. In the momentary reprieve from the absolute chaos, she found herself thinking about her parents, who were supposed to be making the trip in a few days to see her. She hoped they were okay and wished she could find some way to contact them.

Kara fixed her light on the window frame as Jeff started to put the second board into place when they heard a wet thunk coming from the window. Several more thunk, thunk, thunk, thunks followed.

"What in the…" Kara stopped mid-sentence as the light illuminated the glass and the dozen or so slimy clumps affixed to the outside of the window. As Kara approached and put her hand upon the cold glass, a scratching sound resonated, and the glass vibrated mildly. As the duo leaned in to take a closer look they could see beak-like protrusions darting out from the globs, snapping against the glass. Kara removed her hand from the glass and the beaks retracted back into the mollusks.

Kara and Jeff looked at each other briefly in disbelief. Within less than an hour, something had turned their entire existence on its head. The absurdity of the situation was not lost on either of the pair. All the while, the otherworldly sounds pierced through the walls of the building from unknown abominations, both outside and within the hallways of the apartment complex.

Broken from their thoughts, they resumed hurriedly putting the makeshift barrier up on the remaining window, lining the board up so that they had a porthole to see outside. Just as they were putting the finishing touches on the barrier, the ground gently began to shake. The shaking picked up intensity until Jeff thought he could feel his fillings rattling, and then it abruptly stopped.

Kara pointed to the view hole. "Look, the slime balls are falling off."

Jeff peered through the porthole, taking

the flashlight from Kara's outstretched hand and placing it against the window. Sure enough, the mollusk-like snot balls were slowly plopping off of the window. Jeff pressed the light against the window to see if it would pierce beyond the window. Suddenly, he shot back and fell on his backside as if hit by a bolt of lightning, dropping the flashlight during the fall.

"What is it!?" Kara asked.

"Get away from the window," Jeff whispered as he slowly crab walked backwards on the floor, putting distance between himself and the window.

As the light spun on the floor, it briefly illuminated the small opening and Kara gasped. Just outside of the pane of glass, filling the entire view, was a gargantuan, bloodshot eye. The soccer ball sized pupil contracted when the flashlight briefly fell upon it. Kara scrambled to grab and deactivate the flashlight and succeeded after briefly knocking it further across the bedroom floor. The tension in the air hung heavily in the darkness as the survivors held their breath. Jeff closed his eyes, fists clenched, waiting for the exterior wall of his room to be blown out as some giant creature grasped and devoured them. The 30 seconds that Kara and Jeff remained huddled on the floor still as statues, dragged on for what felt like days. The ground once again shook violently, knocking Jeff's wall mounted TV to the floor and spilling the menagerie of junk from his dresser.

The vibrations gradually became fainter, and Jeff slowly stood.

"Ok then, if I seemed on the fence before, I can definitely say now I'm not going outside," Jeff whispered.

Kara was visibly shaking, and she simply responded, "Yeah."

They hadn't noticed during the most recent grim encounter that the pounding at the front door of Jeff's apartment had ceased, but after a few minutes, the absence of the noise dawned on them. The eerie foreign noises continued coming from outside the windows of the apartment, but the banging at the door had fallen silent. "Maybe our hallway guests have given up," Jeff whispered. The slam of another door in the hallway broke the stillness of the corridor.

A man with a deep voice shouted, "What in the hell is going on here? Is anyone else hearin —," before a blood-curdling scream interrupted him. Jeff headed towards the front door, but Kara grabbed him by the arm.

"Don't open the door. There is nothing we can do for him."

The scream descended into a mortifying gurgling sound before ceasing altogether.

The confusion and the scream were horrible enough, but the gurgling made Jeff sick to his stomach. He ground his nails into the palms of his hands and knew that the sound would haunt his nightmares for the rest of his life. His skin crawled with goose flesh. It felt like the room was spinning. *This could not be happening, he thought again. This cannot be real. When am I going to wake up?*

Kara's voice snapped him back to the ever-increasing grisly present. "How many other people live here? We've got to try to warn them."

"Our phones aren't working, these damn freaks are in the building, and we can barely see two feet in front of us with a flashlight. I don't see how we're going to do that," Jeff said distantly.

Kara, exacerbated, retorted, "We have to try. Can't you hear right through the wall to the next apartment when someone is loud? I know I can pretty much hear my neighbor brush his teeth. Maybe we can start there. There's at least two people we can reach from right here, and they each have a neighbor on either side. It's something."

Jeff nodded his head in agreement as he approached the bedroom wall that was shared with the apartment. He began by lightly knocking on it with a fist and speaking in a hushed tone, "Anyone still alive over there?"

He and Kara eagerly waited for a response. After a brief pause, he knocked and spoke a little louder. They paused and waited again.

This time, a muffled male's voice responded from the shared wall, "Stop knocking, and keep your voice down. Something's in my living room."

Jeff whispered back, cupping his hands around his mouth as he did so, "Don't go out there man, do you have anything to defend yourself with over there?"

"No shit genius, and yes, I'm currently holding a sword, and now is not the time to ask why I have a sword," the voice responded.

"Did you get a look at it? How did it get in?" Jeff continued, ignoring the insult.

"I didn't get a look at it, but based on the noises that have been coming from around this place, I don't think I want to. I cracked my living room window open earlier because of how damn hot this place always is. Shortly after the bang, I was looking for a flashlight in my room and these weird sounds started. Then I thought I heard the window moving up in the living room. I put my ear to my bedroom door and heard something thud, dropping from the sill to the floor. Then I could hear clacking, like a dog's claws, on the linoleum and stuff started smashing off my counters. Haven't been out to check, but I can still hear it out there."

"Hang tight and listen for me. We're going to try to figure something out," Jeff said, the determination in his voice belying the anxiety he felt.

CHAPTER EIGHT

Eagerly, the team fixated on the brilliant monitor, casting a glow across their faces as it displayed the robot Crystal controlled. The initial entry flooded the screen with blinding radiance, briefly obscuring their view. Once their vision readjusted, a sleek metallic corridor unfolded before them, its walls gleamed under the artificial illumination. The robot, with its powerful treads, commenced a deliberate advance into the brightly lit passageway, each foot echoing through the suspense-laden atmosphere.

Time seemed to distort while within the craft. The ship was enormous, but the inside could not have been more than 75 yards linear. Although the bomb disarming robot was only chuffing along at a steady five miles per hour, they should have reached the other end of the craft at least five minutes ago. Yet, the corridor seemed to stretch out endlessly.

Patrick, his view homed in on the glowing

monitor, spoke slowly. "This doesn't make a lick of sense. How long have we been inside now?"

Looking at his wristwatch, Scott responded, "Almost 22 minutes now. It's like the thing rolled onto a treadmill."

The only sign that this was not the case was an occasional outline etched into a wall showing what appeared to be a closed door, each of which had no visible handles. Crystal had tried navigating the robot to push the first few of the perceived doors open, but none of them had budged. Now she continued trudging the robot along down the seemingly endless hallway, looking for any openings or visible controls in the great enigma of the ship.

The robot, equipped to record sound, showed that the humming sound coming from the craft was increasing in volume; one of the few indications that the team was making any forward progress. Time and distance morphed into an amalgamation of insanity and vertigo as the team continued to question their own sanity. Condensation accumulated on the inside of their suits' helmets as the group spiraled into what felt like a fever dream.

After several more hours exhaustion took hold of the team, their postures slumped visibly. Crystal's eyes blurred from the monotony, the endless journey within the craft seeming like a trek to nothingness. Her mind wandered, flashing back to the life leading up to this disappointingly pivotal moment. The crowded inner-city apartment where her mother raised her and four siblings, the routine of ushering them home from school, passing stern men in red at the courtyard. Pulling out bread and peanut butter to make five sandwiches for dinner, turning on the TV, and later waiting on the couch for her mom to return after a double shift at the local diner. The experiences motivated her to work harder in school, get a full ride to college, eventually getting her doctorate in biophysics.

As Crystal drifted into memories, the weariness of the present merged with the challenges of her past. The echoes of her childhood struggles resonated within the mind-altering effects of the entity they once perceived as a spacecraft. Now, doubts crept in, questioning whether it was a mere vessel or a portal to another world. The cramped confines intensified the weight of their current plight, and amidst the exhaustion, a spark of resilience flickered, a reminder that the science of pursuing the unknown demanded more than mental fortitude, it required drawing strength from the indomitable spirit forged in the crucible of her life's journey. The memories reinvigorated her to shake the heaviness in her eyes and continue on.

As the robot advanced, the rhythmic resonance of its treads echoed through the metallic corridor. The team, captivated by the monitor's display, watched intently after nearly four hours. It finally approached what appeared to be an end of the hallway. A large metallic door, standing ajar, hinted at mysteries beyond. As the robot reached this threshold, a different colored illumination spilled through the opening, casting an eerie glow that beckoned both curiosity and apprehension.

As Crystal piloted the machine forward, pushing the door fully open, a brief image of the rear of a lone chair mounted atop a steel pole flashed onto the monitor before it was replaced with a black screen.

"What happened?!" Mindy exclaimed, rushing forward to attempt to reboot the monitor.

Pointing to the previously green indicator light on the robot's remote that was now dimmed out, Crystal responded, "I don't know, but I have a feeling it's not coming back."

Scott cut in, visibly irritated. "Son of a bitch, of course, we end up driving inside a damn spacecraft no longer than a football field for what now, four hours!? And as soon as we see anything worth seeing, the stupid piece of shit breaks!"

"I don't think it's the robot, I think this thing doesn't want us getting close to its control center," Patrick calmly countered.

Mindy interjected, "It's a crashed piece of metal over 50 years old that we haven't figured a damn thing out about in just as long. Now you think it's sentient?"

"I don't know what I'm saying, but it clearly

isn't just a hunk of flying metal. How long have we been hunched over this monitor? We could have driven that thing to the city and back by now," Patrick said, gesturing to the control Crystal still held in her hands. "Does that make sense to you? Does any of this make sense to you?" he finished.

Scott and Mindy, in a shared moment of defeat, softly uttered, "No."

Crystal set down the remote and turned to the group. "We've got to go in."

Everyone nodded in agreement, but the reluctance showed on many of their faces.

Patrick spoke, "We're going to need to take some supplies in with us, time and distance are distorted in there, if it took us that long to make it to the end of the hallway with the robot," he paused before finishing his thought, "The last thing we need to do is go in there and starve to death."

Fortunately, the researchers had a well-stocked lab with snacks and bottled water, so the team could minimize leaving the lab once they started their day. This was because of the need to keep their project secret and the inconvenience of going through multiple security checkpoints and keypads on a lunch break. As a result, going out for lunch became a time-consuming task.

The team found two backpacks in a storage closet that contained odds and ends that other researchers had left in the lab over the years and began stocking them with provisions. While packing, Crystal turned to Patrick. "I don't know if you should go in. You've got a family at home, and we don't know what might happen in there. The electromagnetic and radiation levels alone could do god knows what to us."

"I think you're going to need all the help you can get in there and there's no way I'd sit this out. This is a chance at finally understanding what the hell this thing really is. I think one person should stay out here, monitor us from the audio and video in the suits, keep in communication, give us a sense of how long we're in there and maybe point out anything we aren't seeing," Patrick responded.

The steadily elevating humming in the background emphasized the urgency of the team's situation.

"So, who's going with us and who wants to stay and be home base?" Patrick asked.

Scott and Mindy exchanged a nervous look with one another.

"I knew it! I knew when I got the call and headed over here, by the end of the damn day I was gonna end up in that creepy fucking thing. I said to myself. Don't worry Scott, there's four of you, and that useless hunk of metal hasn't done a damn thing since the government recovered it. Why would you have to go in? But here I am, about to volunteer to go in and get fried with you lunatics."

The rest of the team couldn't help but laugh. Scott's anxiety-driven monologues were something they had become accustomed to over the years. Right now, it was a welcome glimmer of normalcy that briefly cut through the grave situation they found themselves in.

The team had worked together for quite some time now. Mindy, being the newest addition, was now in her fourth year in the lab. In most circumstances, they looked forward to spending the day with their counterparts at the lab and working on the complex task charged to them. They were also close outside of work and would frequently have cookouts at Patrick's house or hit a restaurant together, the lab members melding with Patrick's wife and kids into one enormous family. The tight-knit coworkers were like added aunts and uncles to Patrick's two children. If any of them befell harm within the ship, they would all feel the effects reverberate through their lives much more than any workplace condolences email.

"I guess that makes me the command post," Mindy said smiling.

Patrick pointed toward the ship. "We need to stay close, nothing makes sense in there, reality is twisted, and time doesn't seem to move, the last thing we need is someone getting separated from the group and ending up stuck in that thing,"

Crystal gestured toward the bank of meters. "Hopefully, we can cover the distance quicker than the robot did, find some sort of off switch and get right out. If these levels keep rising, someone above our pay grade is going to have to explain why half of Harford County was leveled by something they were doing at APG,"

The team huddled, crafting a strategic plan while meticulously outlining contingency measures. Mindy, at the center, was equipped with essential contacts, primed for unforeseen challenges. A call to the project's military commander reassured them- ongoing surveillance and a commitment to provide necessary resources. Swiftly, two armed soldiers materialized, one joining the entry team, the other poised to support Mindy. The atmosphere buzzed with a palpable blend of anxiety and determination. Fear of the unknown was somehow less terrifying than uncovering it.

The three scientists and lone armed soldier, now outfitted with a suit of his own, stood feet away from the glowing entryway. Their shadows casted off elongated silhouettes on the far wall. Energy pulsating from the craft penetrated the quartet's bones. Crystal had a metallic taste, reminiscent of blood, on the inside of her mouth and her head swam in an ocean of confusion.

"Everyone ready," Patrick asked the soon to be explorers looking over his shoulder. The other three gave a thumbs up belying the fact that they could not have been less ready. Patrick disappeared through the glowing doorway followed by the soldier, Crystal standing on the precipice of the unknown. The unnatural hum of the alien craft reverberated through her being as she hesitated; a moment pregnant with anticipation. The metallic taste lingered, a haunting reminder of the mystery awaiting her on the other side. With a deep breath, Crystal plunged into the luminous portal, her senses overwhelmed by a surreal fusion of colors and sounds. Behind her Scott entered the doorway while muttering obscenities under his breath.

Inside, the air seemed to vibrate with an indescribable energy. Their surroundings were vastly different than what they had witnessed from the monitors. Each step made a small ripple appear on the floor that gently arched outward in a never-ending ring, as if a stone had broken the surface of a still pond. Patrick and the soldier were barely visible ahead, navigating through a seemingly endless corridor. Crystal's steps felt weightless, her every movement synchronized with the pulsating rhythm of the alien realm. The plain hallway that had shown on the robots feed was replaced with pulsing colors.

As they ventured deeper, the shadows of uncertainty grew thicker. Patrick's voice echoed, distorted by the surreal environment. "Stay close. We need to stick together. This looks nothing like what we saw on the drone," he called out, his words carrying an urgency that heightened the tension. Crystal's heart raced, and the metallic taste intensified as if the very air conspired to keep her on edge.

The four moved through the unfamiliar corridor, the walls alive with strange patterns that seemed to pulse in response to their presence. Suddenly, the soldier halted, raising a hand to signal caution. Crystal's breath caught in her throat as they approached a colossal chamber bathed in an ethereal glow. In the center, a pedestal stood with something sitting on top, illuminated by a focused light on the object.

As the explorers gathered at the threshold of this mysterious chamber, a sense of foreboding settled over them. Crystal's mind was racing. This wasn't on the robot's feed. How long had they walked, 30 seconds? She felt an overwhelming sense of vertigo, her eyes unable to focus.

CHAPTER NINE

Mark glanced over his shoulder, his voice cutting through the tension. "Guys, secure this entryway. We're sweeping the rest of this place. Stay vigilant and be ready to let us back in. If I have to sprint back and find you snoozing, I'll haunt your asses if I'm the one who gets eaten."

Two familiar officers, one in tactical gear and jeans, the other having abandoned any law enforcement facade hours ago, clad in a hoodie and sweatpants but armed with an AR, emerged from the shadows. One nodded, and Sweatpants assured, "We've got you covered."

Loki stood by the entrance, eagerly anticipating the removal of the barrier. When the barrier was removed, he could get to work. He loved the games he got to play while with the man, and he loved the man. The man took him everywhere, and he felt courage in the man's presence, even in situations that were scary or loud. The man, his source of comfort, also scratched his belly like he liked and played with him at home with the rest of his pack. Loki knew that whatever was going on was different and the new terrible animals had a distinct smell. Although much different from anything his nose had picked up before, Loki wasn't scared. He would find the bad smells with the man and then he would get to go home and get his chin rubbed by the man. Loki loved his man.

After the lockers were removed, Mark looked at Ken. "Ready?"

Ken nodded, and Loki's tail wagged in excitement. Mark removed the shield doorway and Loki slipped through. Ken and Mark followed, their weapons raised, the under-barrel mount lights feebly cutting into the darkness.

Ken once again said, "Close, Loki," cautioning the dog of excessive excitement and straying far from his side. Loki wasn't just a working partner; he was an integral part of Ken's family. The idea of anything happening to the Malinois weighed on Ken, akin to the concern he would feel for a human family member facing harm. In other departments, Ken had met handlers who viewed their dogs as tools, deploying them without regard for the risks, especially against armed individuals. Ken, however, never saw Loki in this utilitarian light and would never callously expose him to unnecessary danger.

Ken, with a stoic exterior that concealed his true emotions, would never openly admit to another person the depth of his love for Loki. To his colleagues, he kept a tough image, a man of few words, but beneath that rugged exterior was an unspoken bond that transcended the typical handler-dog relationship. Loki, with his keen instincts, sensed the unspoken affection and reciprocated it with unwavering loyalty. In the silence of their partnership, emotions spoke louder than words ever could.

The two men followed Loki's lead, knowing that the dog's keen sense of smell would lead them to the nearest threat. As the trio padded along at a fast walk, Ken routinely reminded his fur partner to stay close. The shrieks and screams of distant monstrosities from outside the building played an erratic, bone chilling tune the whole while.

After hearing a particularly long moan, Mark muttered, "I should have fuckin retired, could be sitting home drinking a rum and coke on my back deck right now instead of trying to die in this dump with you."

"You think this craziness is isolated to the city? I don't buy that, plus you live, what, five miles from here?" Ken retorted.

"I didn't say that. I said I could sit on my back deck drinking, and I stand by that. End of the world darkness filled with monsters, still could drink on my deck, least I'd give one of these things a hangover when they ate me," Mark said.

Ken chuckled and appreciated Mark's dark humor making light of the terror they both felt.

The trio came to the closed stairwell door. The officers knew that it held a single flight of stairs that led up to the commanders' offices and a few administrative storage rooms. Loki sat in front of the closed door and turned to look at Ken. "Good boy Loki," Ken said, patting the dog on his head.

Ken pressed his ear against the door, the frigid touch of metal briefly tempering the searing anticipation he experienced countless times. It was the precarious moment before confronting a door, harboring an imminent threat, demanding his attention. Where he and his fellow officers were the only thing left to deal with whatever horrible situation had reached its pinnacle, that prompted someone to call the police. He never got used to the feeling but had long ago learned to mold the fear, use it to sharpen his instincts rather than hamper them.

Every sight, sound, smell, and touch amplified. He had observed others who could not control the fear make terrible life-altering decisions and had attended the funerals of some who had paid the ultimate price due to their inability to control it. This wasn't to say that an officer giving the ultimate sacrifice was the fault of their own. Many finer men and women had just been the unlucky recipient of horrible circumstances that were beyond their control, but it was a risk factor.

Ken turned to Mark and whispered, "Hear that?" A muffled noise like a distant conversation sounded on the other side of the door. Ken steeled himself-not waiting for a response, he said,

"Opening."

Decades of training rendered making entry to buildings second nature. Ken, positioned beside the door, gently eased it ajar with his foot, his senses alert to every creak and rustle. Mark, attuned to the subtlest movements, methodically cleared the visible space. The duo prepared for a dynamic entry, Ken advancing cautiously, Mark swift on his heels, mentally dividing the stairwell into sections, each step resonating with tension.

The landing appeared clear of any immediate threats. Thin strands of cobwebs floated through the air, catching on Ken's head and upper body, giving him the creepy sensation of being crawled on by minute insects. Loki let out a low growl, and they heard the muffled speaking again coming from up the first set of steps. As they progressed upward cautiously, limited by the short distance that their flashlights pierced the darkness. The racket increased.

Halfway up the set of stairs, Ken's light fell upon a disturbing scene. What appeared to be a giant spider web encompassed the stairwell wall above their heads and contained a menagerie of disgust. Large white sacks, some of them containing puncture marks that oozed a dark substance, clung to the surface of the web. The muffled speaking was coming from one sac that was writhing in the wall's corner.

"Oh my god," Mark muttered.

Ken's mind was racing as he tried to conjure

an image of what unseen horror had painted the morbid canvas he was staring at. With what he had witnessed thus far in the night, he had little doubt it would be straight out of a sadist's worst nightmare. His skin crawled as more of the fine strands of web tickled his face. He tried to control the growing fear from taking over and pushing him into panic mode as they ascended a few more steps. Sweat was beading on his forehead despite the cold outside air penetrating the poorly heated station. He felt the heaviness of bearing the shotgun burning in his shoulders and neck.

They scanned the wall and ceiling as far as their lights could penetrate, searching for the creator of the repulsive display. As the grotesque sack continued to squirm and make a preening sound, a chittering began from outside the reach of the lights. Loki's growl increased, joining the symphony of madness within the enclosed stairwell. Ken and Mark stood in tense anticipation, their weapons poised and aimed towards the mysterious origin of the unnerving sound. A shiver ran down their spines as they braced themselves, the oppressive darkness concealing the impending revelation that lurked just beyond their trembling grasp.

Ken, in the wake of his gruesome encounters thus far, was starting to feel immune to the horrors emerging from the shadows, he was convinced that no atrocity could surprise him anymore. Yet again, he was wrong. He would not have been surprised had a giant mutated spider came forth from the darkness, but as the creature emerged into the beam of their lights, he felt an urge to vomit.

It was a nightmare conjured up from the depths of hell. A human-esque figure with an additional set of arm like protuberances, a face with bloodshot, emerald green eyes stared at the men from a sunken face filled with dozens of jagged oversized teeth. There was nothing resembling the human idea of skin present on the abomination. Visible fibers of red muscles and ligaments contracted and flexed as it let out a chilling roar before skittering across the web to bite into the writhing sack. A dark-colored rain spattered down on the trio. The rain intensified, taking on an unnatural viscosity as it cascaded down. The entity, now adorned with the dripping remnants of its macabre feast, continued its skittering dance across the web. The blood-soaked fibers of its muscles seemed to writhe in anticipation, pulsating with an unholy energy. Both men, momentarily paralyzed with terror, felt the warm touch of the blood rain seeping into their clothing, a relentless reminder of the malevolent force that lurked beyond the veil of human understanding.

Mark let out a low gasp that was instantly drowned out by the explosion of Ken's 12-gauge. Mark instantly added to the banging echoes in the stairwell by unloading his service weapon.

The unnatural sounds of the world outside of the station were monetarily drowned out by a mixture of deafening booms and the metallic clinking of spent shell casings littering the floor.

Loki added to the thundering chaos by barking furiously while leaping off the ground and snapping his jaws, well out of reach of the creature. One of the monstrosities' six arms disintegrated in a mist of black-colored liquid and gore. The creature let out a blood-curdling shriek and leaped from its perch, while a thick silk strand protruding from its back kept it connected to the web. It descended in a flash, seizing hold of the k9 with two of its distorted appendages. Loki let out a surprised yelp before violently trying to grab hold of the arms gripping him.

CHAPTER TEN

In the softly lit kitchen, Jeff and Kara rummaged through their stash, quietly discussing plans to rescue the newfound neighbor next door. Amidst the cans and provisions, Kara shot a puzzled glance at Jeff. "Our phones and cable are dead, but the lights are still on. What gives?" she asked, unpacking supplies from her backpack.

Jeff, setting down a can, explained, "The place has backup generators- a perk I never really thought about until now."

Kara, absorbing the revelation, continued unloading. "Okay, but how long can these generators keep running? We can't rely on this forever." The room seemed to echo with unease as they confronted the unpredictable limits of their sanctuary.

In the gloomy kitchen, Jeff surveyed their meager arsenal of supplies with a hint of uncertainty. "Predicting how long these generators will last is a guessing game," he confessed, motioning toward the matches, candles, and manual can opener. "We've got some basics covered, but we'll be good for a bit. I doubt we're going to find anywhere else with power."

Jeff shifted his focus to the immediate challenge at hand. "That guy next door is stuck with that thing in his kitchen, and I don't like our chances with those things in the hall. I hit that thing with everything I had with a freaking baseball bat, and it barely lost a beat."

Kara, ever resourceful, leaned against the counter, deep in thought. "The walls are thin," she observed, her mind racing with possibilities. "What if we create an opening? We could get him through to our side, then we can find a way to seal the opening. Or we all go for the thing in his kitchen, three-on-one."

The idea dangled in the space, a fragile thread of hope. Jeff considered it, weighing the risks and rewards. "It's risky, but it might be our best shot. Let's open the wall. I don't think we'll make it in the hallway. We need to act fast before whatever's in his kitchen figures out he's there." The urgency in his voice underscored the precariousness of their situation.

Determined, they returned to the bedroom. Jeff lightly tapped on the wall and whispered, "Hey man, you there?"

The man's voice returned, "I'm kind of limited in my options of places to go because of the beast in my kitchen, and the name's Carl."

"I'm Jeff. We think we have an idea. What if we make a hole in the wall and get you over here?"

"The only problem I see with that is the

thing doesn't know I'm in here yet. If we make a ton of noise bashing in the wall, what's keeping it from knocking down the bedroom door and following me right through?"

"Maybe, but if it did, it would have to deal with three of us. Otherwise, you're just waiting for it to figure out you're there."

"Alright, guess it would be less lonely to get eaten with my neighbors," Carl responded, a glimmer of humor in his voice.

Jeff found a serrated kitchen knife he figured he could use as a drywall saw. His dad had showed him some basic drywall repair as a kid so he knew the basic layout. He knew that there would be a layer of drywall, fiberglass insulation and then another layer of Carl's drywall. With a sense of urgency, he tried to pinpoint the spaces devoid of wooden studs by lightly tapping the wall, listening for the hollow sound. He wanted to avoid the need for restarts that could shatter Carl's impromptu hiding spot.

Jeff's hands trembled as he worked to create a hole in the wall. Each stroke of the knife sent a chill down his spine. He focused on the task at hand, periodically updating Carl, "We're almost there. Just a bit more."

Behind the wall, Carl's hushed voice conveyed the unfolding horror. "It sounds like it's in the living room, but it's moving around."

The distant sounds of the living room moved closer, a scraping noise resonated, it was back onto the linoleum floor of the kitchen. Carl's breath caught as he relayed, "It's getting closer. Stay quiet."

As the hole widened inch by inch, anxiety permeated the atmosphere like a thick fog. Carl, now visible through the gap, looked back with a mix of fear and anticipation. "Hurry up, guys."

Carl's voice crackled with fear. "It's right outside the door, sniffing around. Be quiet." Jeff froze mid sawing. The beast on the other side seemed to sense the disturbance, its predatory instincts on high alert.

Carl whispered again, "Quiet, quiet. It's trying the door."

Jeff sawed as fast as he could while trying to stifle the noise. If the thing already sensed that Carl was in the room, then they needed to get him out now.

A thumping started at Carl's bedroom door. Carl, using his hands, began tearing chunks of drywall from his side of the wall, widening the gap. The thumping at the door intensified as they frantically scrambled to widen the opening enough for Carl to squeeze through. Perspiration accumulated on Jeff's palms, making him periodically slip on the knife. His forearms were on fire from the repetitive exertion.

Carl's panicked voice cut through the sawing. "The door's starting to splinter!"

Suddenly, a baseball sized hole blasted into Carl's bedroom door. Carl watched with growing horror as an oversized black eye filled the opening, peering at his spot on the bed. The eye moved away from the new hole and was replaced by a long skeletal arm equipped with four, long, twig thin fingers searching for the handle. "Okay guys, I'm squeezing my ass through here right now! Watch your faces!" Carl shouted, pushing his sword through the opening first.

Carl snuck a glance over his shoulder before putting his head through the opening. He saw that the creature's long fingers, not agile enough to disengage the lock on the door, had reverted to violently shaking the door with one abnormal arm gripping the handle through the hole it had made. Despite pushing with all his strength, Carl found himself trapped at his broad shoulders. He violently thrashed in tandem with the door behind him, attempting to fit through the new passageway. Jeff hurriedly began breaking away more of the drywall around the edges of the wall. Carl soon had one of his shoulders in the opening. They could hear the hinges of the door beginning to rattle. Sweat poured down his face from the mixture of fear and exertion, drywall dust clung to the perspiration and his dark hair.

His second shoulder had just made it through the wall when he heard the crash of the door hitting the floor. A scrambling struggle started behind him as the creature freed its trapped arm from beneath the door. Carl's legs were shooting through the wall while Jeff and

Kara pulled his large, muscular arms from the other side. The audible snapping of hungry jaws was now inches from his feet. Carl fell through to salvation of Jeff's mattress as the creature's grotesque head followed through the hole in the wall. The trio jumped back as the chomping jaws narrowly missed taking a piece of Carl's foot. The monster's arms scratched the opposite side of the wall, too wide to fit into the opening.

Momentarily frozen, Jeff stared at the horrendous thrashing thing stuck in his wall. Large black eyes, all pupils, stared back at him. A face that could have resembled a human in another world, but more beast than person. Long needle teeth protruded from a maw that made up half of the being's face snapped over and over. Where a nose should have been were two slits that oozed clear slime. Jeff noticed in his daze that small chunks of gristle were lodged in between its teeth. An icy shiver ran through Jeff. This had not been the creature's first human contact, and it appeared that the last person didn't fare as well as Jeff and his newfound friends. Kara's shouts were distant and muffled, indecipherable in Jeff's current fugue.

As the creature's grotesque form became more apparent under the dim lighting, Carl, with his imposing stature and intense dark eyes, took a firm stance, readying his sword. His muscled physique, honed from years of physical labor, was a blur as it pushed by Jeff. In an instant Carl drove the tip of his sword through the forehead of the monster and just as quickly retracted it with an audible squelch. The beast went limp, dripping a foul-smelling liquid onto the bed.

"Sorry man, I don't think that stain's coming out," Carl jested, making light of the group's horrifying situation. Carl placed a booted foot on the face of the creature and shoved it back through the hole. The springs of his mattress groaned with the weight of the thing's body.

Jeff returned to reality, breaking his silence. "Should we try to seal this hole?"

"Or we go through, get the window in Carl's living room shut and barricade his apartment, too. Then we can check for survivors next to his place," Kara suggested.

"Not a bad plan, as long as nothing else has made its way through the window by now," Carl responded.

"There's three of us now, and apparently these things aren't impervious to dying," Kara said, motioning towards Carl's sword.

Jeff nodded his head slowly in agreement. "We should probably try to get that thing out of your room, too. Who knows what diseases we might catch if it festers over there for however long we're stuck here?"

After removing the box spring from Jeff's bed they placed it against the new opening between the apartments. The group convened around Jeff's modest kitchen table, the distant alien sounds reverberated from the outside and hallways of the apartment.

Carl showed his stash of materials, acquired through his weekend gig as a handyman, proposing a plan to fortify windows and doors. Unanimously, they resolved to begin by securing Carl's contiguous living space, and disposing of the creature's remains somehow. Subsequently, their strategy involved reaching out to the neighbor opposite Carl's unit. The group envisioned crafting a makeshift barrier for the aperture connecting Carl and Jeff's apartments, utilizing Jeff's space for rest and meals while leveraging Carl's as a hub for contacting neighboring residents.

"After we check next door, we can check the apartments above and below. God knows I can hear the upstairs neighbor blow his nose with these damn thin walls," Carl remarked.

"Yeah, but we need to tread lightly. Most of these things can probably get through just as easily. The exterior and hallway walls are brick, but if one of the apartments has one of those creatures inside, they're just as likely to burst through as another survivor is," Jeff responded.

"True, we can use some of the interior doors from my apartment to fortify any holes we make," Carl suggested.

As they discussed their strategy, Carl's brown eyes flickered with concern, his thoughts wandering beyond the immediate crisis. In the weekday hours, he toiled at a local grocery store, navigating the mundane aisles and interacting with regular customers. His familiarity with basic carpentry, a skill honed during weekends as a handyman, now emerged as a valuable asset.

Amidst the conversation, a worried expression crossed Carl's face, and he hesitated before voicing a question that had been gnawing at him. "I can't shake the worry about Ash," he confessed, referring to his girlfriend living on the other side of town. "I wonder if she's safe, dealing with whatever's happening out there." The unspoken anxiety lingered in the air.

Kara, sitting across the table, nodded pensively. "I get that, Carl. I'm worried too. My family's across the state in Pittsburgh, and I haven't been able to reach them. This whole situation is a nightmare, and we're not alone in feeling that way." The shared concern for loved ones further intensified the direness of their situation. Jeff remained silent but nodded his head in agreement, thinking of his parents in the northern part of the state.

The trio made their way back to the bedroom and stood nervously before the box spring they had used to plug the hole in the wall, steeling themselves for their next move. As the group removed the box spring from the opening, the overpowering stench of the beast's corpse assaulted their senses.

"Ah, man, that smells like shit," Jeff exclaimed, hastily covering his nose with his shirt. The pungent odor lingered in the air, a stark reminder of the peril they faced. The next revelation came as amplified, monstrous sounds emanated from the outside world.

Simultaneously, a gentle breeze, presumably from the open window in Carl's living room, wafted into his now doorless bedroom and through the opening. Despite the foreboding ambiance, Carl, showing a mix of determination and caution, was the first to venture through the opening. He had volunteered, acknowledging that it was his apartment, and his sword had already proven to be an effective line of defense. The anticipation of what lay beyond heightened as the group followed Carl into the unknown. The lingering echoes of distant horrors underscoring their advance.

As Carl led the way through the opening, Jeff followed closely, gripping his baseball bat with tense determination. The transition from one apartment to another felt like crossing a threshold into an unknown realm. Behind them, Kara trailed cautiously, clutching a kitchen knife- a makeshift, but necessary defense.

Each member of the group had to step over the grotesque corpse of the slain monster sprawled across Carl's bed. The creature's presence served as a grim reminder of the dangers they faced. As they moved forward, the strange sounds from the open window in Carl's living room merged with the echoing roars of the monsters outside, creating a horrifying symphony that permeated the air.

Approaching where Carl's door now lay on the floor, the group listened intently for any signs of movement within the apartment. The cacophony from outside made it challenging to discern subtle sounds within the confines of Carl's home. The trio exchanged wary glances; their senses heightened as they waited to move beyond the perceived safety of the room.

CHAPTER ELEVEN

Crystal stared in a state of reverie. "How is this possible, the drone? It went for hours. We've barely made it inside. How?"

Patrick, shaking his head, slowly responded, "I think it wanted us to find this room. Whatever is atop that podium, it's for us."

Anger masking his fear, Scott interjected, "No, no, no, something between the electromagnetic and radiation levels made the robots video play on a loop so we thought we were seeing an endless hallway, which could have happened, because this, this isn't possible. It's a ship. It can't just change rooms and walls and structures, it just can't."

Mindy chimed in over the group's headsets, "I'm seeing exactly what you are right now guys, and to confirm, same time out here you've been in there less than a minute."

Patrick spoke in a hushed tone, "Scott, this goes well beyond anything we perceive to be reality. Think about it, we know no living beings are within light years of our planet, yet this thing landed here in the 50s, we hadn't even landed on the moon yet, for Christ sakes the first weather satellite wasn't even launched until 1960, whatever we're dealing with here is advanced beyond our understanding. It wasn't the bomb robot running on a loop Scott, it wanted us to come in, it wanted us to find this room."

Scott cupped his stubbled chin, and slowly shook his head.

Crystal took a step forward. "He's right Scott, I know it goes against every logical fiber in your body, but I can feel it. It wanted us to come in, it wanted us to find this room. Maybe it did project a loop on the robot, but it wasn't the energy levels. Whether it's the ship, or there's still an occupant somewhere aboard, in control of all of this, this was planned."

Struggling with the incongruity of the situation, Scott shouted before trailing off, "No, it can't! It just doesn't add up"

Crystal placed a hand on Scott's shoulder and softly spoke, "I know it doesn't buddy, either way let's deal with what's in front of us, let's figure out what's on that stand."

The soldier, a fearless, disciplined man named Kurt, had listened to the first part of the conversation between the scientists before tuning them out. He was busy assessing the chamber for any visible threats and egress points. Kurt had come from a long lineage of brave Americans who had served in the United States Army. Protecting others, freedom, and a love for his country ran through his veins. Kurt knew the scientists were the best bet at deactivating this "ticking time bomb", as his commanding officer had put it, but right now they were bickering over nonsense as far as he was concerned. He was here on direct orders to safely escort the researchers in finding a way to shut this thing down and while they were busy arguing over philosophy, he was busy making sure no big-eyed ETs jumped their asses. As he tuned back into the conversation, he heard the last few words Crystal had spoken to Scott. Having stepped further into the corridor than the others to ensure the podium wasn't some sort of IED, he responded, "It's a book."

"A book?" Patrick asked curiously.

"Yeah, just a big ass book. The cover has something written on it, but it's no language I've ever seen. Any of you want to take a look?" Kurt responded, looking over the group of researchers.

Crystal was the first to make it to Kurt's side by the mammoth red leather-bound book. "You think it's safe to pick up?"

"As far as I can see there're no wires or anything else indicating it's a trap, but with whatever we're dealing with here I couldn't be certain. I mean, we are in a spaceship, aren't we?" Kurt responded by raising his brows at Crystal.

Patrick and Scott had gathered around the

book and were eyeing the gold, slanted characters on its cover curiously. "I can't speak many languages, but I've seen quite a few, and that doesn't look like anything I know of," Patrick said.

"Well, let's open it up," Crystal said, reaching to turn the cover, being careful to leave it on the podium.

The tension between the foursome was palpable as they awaited for her to slowly close the inches between her hand and the book. Scott squeezed his eyes shut in anticipation of the entire room being engulfed in flames, Kurt scanned the room waiting for legions of little green men to spill from the walls at Crystal's touch.

As Crystal gripped the cover and slowly turned it over, a collective sigh of relief was heard among the group when they didn't explode or disintegrate. A sense of awe replaced the relief as they stared at the opening pages of the book. Hundreds of thousands of small glowing circles danced on the pages, emitting hues of colors from every spectrum of the rainbow, and some inarticulable to the human mind, reflected off of the faceplates of the observer's suits. Crystal removed a small glass apparatus, similar to a magnifying glass, from a cutout that was made in the reverse side of the cover.

"What is it?" Kurt asked in a daze.

"It's a sliver of the universe, it's more than we ever imagined. Look here, this is our galaxy," Crystal said, pointing to a small section of glowing clusters on the second page of the open book. She placed the glass over the familiar shape of the Milky Way, and it magically zoomed in, showing intense detail of the various planets and stars within it.

"This is unbelievable, we have estimates based on the Hubble telescope that tell us that there are probably hundreds of billions of galaxies in the universe but we don't know the makeup of them. We're going off of glimmers of light millions of light years away, this is a detailed star by star snapshot of, I don't even know how many, galaxies," Patrick said to no one in particular.

The scientists pondered over these opening pages for several minutes before Kurt reminded them, "Hey guys, this is all awesome and those lights are awful pretty, but we're trying to find a way to shut this thing down, right? Think we could turn a few pages and see if there's anything there in your astrology book about that? I'll keep trying to make sure no creepy crawlies sneak up on us, but if this whole thing detonates, I don't think that matters?"

Crystal nodded her head, "Right, we can take this with us. Let's see if it has anything about the ship in it first though."

Turning to the next page, it was the same map, but now some planets were dark, and some of the planets within the galaxies had a pink ring around them as if circled by a supernatural highlighter. "What the hell..." Scott said.

"Look here's earth, we've got the pink ring around us. What do you think it means?" Crystal asked.

"Your guess is as good as mine, turn the page," Patrick said puzzled.

As Crystal turned to the next page, the group, aside from Kurt, who was still scanning the room, stared, intrigued by the pages. The next page held a diagram, alien characters written above the zigzagging lines of the enigmatic schematics. It looked as if someone had taken a pen and had narrowly failed at covering the entire two pages. Lines zigged, zagged, and overlapped in multiple places.

Trying to trace one of the lines from one end of the page to the other, Crystal lost her place several times before throwing her hands in the air. "Well, this certainly helps clear everything up," she said sarcastically. She placed the looking glass at the start of one of the lines and, in vivid detail, they saw a yellow landscape. The supposed photographer of the scene stood in a wide-open area with tall yellow plants surrounding an open field. The plants were unidentifiable, this coupled with the yellow sky, told the scientists that the snapshot they were viewing was that of another world, and not one identified to be within their solar system. In the center of the field was a clearing. On its borders sat five gargantuan slate black boulders, a stark contrast to the yellow landscape. In the center of the boulders sat the base of a familiar structure, surrounded by advanced scaffolding. It was the base of the ship, or at least an identical ship to the one they found themselves in.

"My god is this the origin of the craft?" Scott asked.

"Maybe not ours," Crystal responded, deftly moving the viewer to the starting point of another line. A pristine snow-covered mountain filled the viewing glass, the only sign that the picturesque scene was not from their planet, the two small suns reflecting off of the icy surface. Once again in the center view of the photo scaffolding, this time less of the craft had been constructed and five ice covered tree tops poking through the snowy landscape ringed the construction in place of the boulders from the earlier site.

"How many lines are there on this diagram? 200, 300 thousand, more? If each one of them represents a ship, a site, how many places have they gone? This is amazing," Patrick exclaimed.

"Put that thing on the end of the line over here," Scott said, pointing to the opposite side of the page.

Crystal lifted the viewing apparatus and placed it on the terminating end of one line. "So this should probably show the destination then," she said.

Shocked exhalations resounded from the group as a dark tableau filled the viewer. Sharp black rock formations jutted from the ground, dimly lit from above by red stars shining in the night sky. A hideous creature was the focal point of the image. Barely visible in the dimly lit world, jet black, it was a slight shade darker than the background night sky. Its misshapen clawed foot stood atop a gory limbless sack of meat. Spindly twisted legs led to a forward tilted pelvis that lacked any distinguishing anatomy that pointed to the sex of the beast. A distended belly met an elongated torso adorned with irregularly long, barely visible arms melded into the darkness. Its face, concealed partially by shadow aside from a yellow toothed smiling mouth stained with a dark liquid that didn't take a scientist to identify. Its yellow eyes were the most visible part of the creature, glowing through the obscureness of the shadows. At the top of its pitch-black hairless head protruded two crooked mismatching horns that both ended in points, also visibly stained with dark liquid. In the upper corner of the scene was more of the alien scribble, possibly a description of the realm by the authors of the book.

"What in the hell is that thing? It looks like a freaking demon—clearly a photograph, not an illustration," Scott whispered, his voice barely audible amidst the tense atmosphere. As the group huddled together, their eyes locked on the disturbing image, a shudder ran down Scott's spine. "I've never seen anything like this before," he added, the unease clear in his expression. The room seemed to tighten with an unspoken fear as they grappled with the enigma captured in the photograph.

Crystal moved the viewer randomly to other endpoints of the diagram quickly, catching glimpses of the various worlds. Some contained beautiful, serene looking locations, others horrible ominous looking places, all clearly unique to one another. Some locations had no living beings in the photos, some had seemingly benign looking alien creatures, others contained variations of creatures only conjured up in the darkest nightmares. One scene contained a horrendous giant holding a horse-like creature suspended in the air above its open mouth, the horse pinched between two giant fingers with a look of terror on its face.

The looking glass fell upon another terminating line. The island where the government found the ship in 1956 filled the looking glass.

CHAPTER
TWELVE

Ken felt his heart skip erratically. The sight of the alien creature clutching his dearest friend was the most terrifying thing Ken had observed tonight. Ken's mind swam. He felt the compounding effects of nonstop adrenaline mixed with exhaustion all reaching their pinnacle as he watched Loki struggling within the grasp of the creature. Memories of him and the Malinois flashed before his watering eyes. He knew he couldn't take a shot with the 12 gauge or he risked the buckshot hitting his partner.

Ken remembered the moment the little black ball of fur first grabbed onto the cuff of his jeans, growling and tugging, choosing him before he even had a chance to examine the litter at the working dog breeding center. The relief he had felt when he returned from the hospital with Sarah and the newborn Grant and Loki had sniffed the child's head and laid a big sloppy dog kiss on him. The countless times the dog had saved his ass, both professionally and personally, when the dog would force his head under Ken's chin when he sensed Ken's PTSD was rearing its ugly head. He felt an unfathomable pit of despair open inside him as he nearly collapsed to the ground.

Just as the freak began to ascend with Loki still in its clutches, undoubtedly going to add to its gruesome collection, a smoking hole opened in the creature's head. The beast lost its grip on Loki and the dog dropped to the ground, sprinting to Ken's side. The monster, no longer with a functioning brain, slowly descended from its silk strand, still attached and wetly thudded to the ground.

"Mark, thank God, that was one hell of a shot. You have no idea how much we owe you," Ken spoke, relief washing over his face.

"I asked for your help. It'd be pretty shitty of me to let that ugly son of a bitch eat your dog," Mark replied.

Ken and Mark, bloodstains on their faces, ascended a few more stairs, their focus on clearing the police station of the unknown monstrosities that lurked within. However, their determined advance came to an abrupt halt as they encountered an imposing obstacle—a dense wall of the monster's web blocking their path. Undeterred, Ken extended the shotgun's barrel, pressing it against the silk barricade to gauge its solidity.

"That's some sturdy shit. I don't think we're getting through this," Ken declared, his frustration palpable. Straining against the resilient silk, he wrestled the shotgun barrel free. Mark, beside him, exchanged a grim nod, acknowledging the futility of their situation.

"If we backtrack, we can take the elevator. We already cleared that section of hallway anyway," Mark said.

Ken's agreement manifested with a nod as they descended the steps, the shrieks and growls of alien sounds still reverberating from the outside. The trio had grown desensitized to the sinister background track beyond the station walls, their ears finely attuned to the subtlest noises within the echoing hallways and rooms. Despite having previously cleared the path toward the elevator, an air of uncertainty shrouded each corner, keeping them on edge.

Ken, acutely aware of time slipping away, quickened his pace. Thoughts of Sarah and Grant, his family waiting at home, gnawed at him. *What the hell am I doing? There are other guys here who could be handling this. The civilians in the roll call room can fend for themselves for a few hours he thought, questioning his role in this nightmarish scenario.*

Sarah, resilient and bright, had the skills of a survivor, but the thought lingered in Ken's mind. The sudden shift in reality had unleashed horrors beyond human comprehension. A chilling image seared into Ken's mind–one of the colossal creatures he had met earlier, casually tearing the roof off his suburban home in search of tempting morsels shaped like his wife and toddler son.

As they traversed the dimly lit corridors, Loki took the lead once more. Seemingly unfazed by his earlier brush with death, quick to forget the bad in life, as most good dogs were. The dog sniffed the air diligently, his heightened senses detecting any lingering presence of the grotesque creatures. The trio moved with a shared tension, a mix of urgency and dread, advancing towards the elevator.

They reached the elevator, their flashlights struggling to pierce the enveloping darkness. The impending arrival at the elevator was signaled not by their limited beams, but by an unexpected obstacle—a potted plant that nearly tripped them a few feet from the looming doors. As they approached, the feeble glow revealed the eerie stillness of the hallway.

A sudden rustling from across the hall prompted them to raise their weapons. Muscles tensed. Yet, an unusual calm settled over them as they realized Loki remained composed, neither growling nor barking at whatever was approaching. The tense atmosphere lingered until another figure emerged from the shadows– Lamont, a fellow officer who, despite being on leave, had rushed through the blinding darkness.

Lamont's sudden arrival sparked a mix of relief and surprise. Ken, who had known Lamont for several years, always held a deep respect for the fellow officer's unwavering dedication to helping others. Despite being relatively new on the force, Lamont had quickly earned a reputation as one of the smartest officers in the precinct. Ken had often found himself impressed by Lamont's quick thinking and problem-solving skills, qualities that were highlighted by his making it to the station alive.

Ken recalled many instances where Lamont's intelligence and resourcefulness had made a significant impact, turning challenging situations in their favor. It wasn't just about the job for Lamont; it was a genuine commitment to the well-being of others that defined him. Ken thought back to precarious situation where a subject had shot a man and after failing to outrun the responding officers had taken another man hostage. After a several hour standoff Lamont, still a rookie, had showed up. Somehow, miraculously he had convinced the guy to drop his weapon and surrender. Ken along with everyone else on the scene were awe struck, Ken had respected him ever since.

As they stood in the dimly lit hallway, Ken couldn't help but appreciate Lamont's tenacity in rushing through the darkness to offer help. The unexpected reunion in the face of chaos only amplified Ken's respect for the man. Ken found solace in having Lamont by their side, knowing that in this nightmarish scenario, Lamont's intellect and determination would be valuable assets.

Lamont informed them of the events leading to his arrival at the station on his day off. Lamont's phone devoid of reception, his power out, he recounted the harrowing journey from his townhome that was only a few blocks away. He had been driven to action by indescribable sounds echoing outside his home and the delayed return of his roommate from work. His flashlight revealed haunting scenes along the way—a fallen man being devoured by a monstrous seven-foot-tall creature, an elongated and skinless figure with an appalling, smiling mouth filled with razor-sharp teeth. Lamont fired his Glock, momentarily driving off the creature, but the man it had attacked lay eviscerated and lifeless.

Entering the station, Lamont connected with the guards at the barricade and got filled in on the current situation. After hearing that Ken had been the one to step up and help Mark clear the station, Lamont rushed to catch them, knowing that Ken probably needed to get home to check on his family.

"Listen, if y'all are good with it, I think I should head with you to clear out the rest of this place," Lamont said, gesturing towards Mark. He finished looking at Ken. "And you get out of here. Get home to your wife and boy. We've got this."

"Thank you brother, don't let this old guy get you killed," Ken said smirking towards Mark before saying, "You two be safe, if we all make it out of this I owe you both a happy hour or two. Me and Loki are going to top off at the armory and hit the road."

Lamont and Mark's reassurances echoed through the dimly lit station, the weight of their camaraderie tangible in the air. Mark, holding out a pair of keys to Ken, said, "Here, take these. If there are any commanders left to chew me out, they'll probably have bigger problems to sort out than missing equipment."

With a nod of appreciation, Ken accepted the keys to the spare Bearcat, the armored vehicle that would hopefully provide a safer journey through the perilous night.

"It might be slower than your cruiser, Ken, but it's a tank on wheels. Better chance against those creatures out there. It will at least give them a stomachache if they eat the whole thing," Mark quipped, his attempt at humor underscoring the gravity of the situation.

A handshake and half-hug exchanged; Ken expressed his gratitude once more before swiftly making his way to the armory. As he approached the door, the sight of the sign-out sheet struck him as absurdly out of place amidst the chaos. A laugh escaped him, a brief respite from the tension that hung thick in the air.

Inside the armory, Ken moved with practiced efficiency, grabbing an AR-15, additional ammunition for his shotgun and handgun, and a spare bulletproof vest. The absence of protective gear for his loyal K9 companion, Loki, didn't escape Ken's notice. "Typical department oversight," he muttered, voicing his frustration.

After securing the bulletproof vest to Loki, hoping it would provide an additional layer of protection from any freakish claws or teeth, Ken headed toward the rear exit door, the distant sounds of monstrous shrieks serving as a reminder of the challenges that awaited him. Each step carried a weight, a mixture of urgency and the acknowledgment that the path ahead was fraught with peril.

As Ken waited by the rear exit door, he felt the familiar grip of his weapons, the reassurance of their presence in the face of the unknown. He and Loki had a 25-yard sprint to the other end of the lot where the Bearcat sat in the open vehicle bay. Ken sent a quick prayer up, asking for the pathway to the vehicle to be clear of any man-eating creatures from another world.

He looked down at Loki and asked, "Ready boy?"

Loki looked back, wagging his tail, affirming that yes, he was in fact ready. Ken hesitated with his hand on the handle for a moment before quickly slamming the door open and started a full-blown sprint towards the vehicle. Loki hung by his side at a steady gallop. Ken braced himself for an unseen impact as he ran in step with the mystifying animal-like shrieks that seemed to surround him. A sliver of relief entered his mind as his flashlight lit up the open garage door of the vehicle bay. Next, the black bumper of the rolling fortress came into view. Ken hit the key fob and briefly worried that the battery would be dead, a common problem for the Bearcat due to all the accessories that drained its power. As he saw the parking lights briefly flash, full blown happiness washed over him. Finally, something was going right amidst the chaotic night.

Ken reached the driver's door of the imposing machine and swung it open. Loki shot past him into the cabin of the vehicle and Ken followed, slamming the door. Ken, now within the relative safety of the castle on wheels, expelled a gust of air from his mouth, a brief release of the anxiety and exhaustion that had built up over the past few hours of trepidation. He knew he had a long journey ahead of him through the streets overrun with unknown horrors.

He gripped the wheel tightly for a second, asked Loki, "Ready to go get Mommy and the boy?"

Loki's ears perked up at this, Ken turned the ignition and the formidable vehicle roared to life. Ken slammed the dash control into drive and began rolling into the eerie blackness.

CHAPTER THIRTEEN

Jeff, Carl, and Kara stood listening for several minutes before Jeff whispered, "I don't hear anything. Now or never." He slowly slipped through the doorway separating the living room from Carl's kitchen. Carl and Kara were right behind him through the doorway. As their lights slowly revealed the kitchen, they observed that it was in complete disarray. The cupboard's contents were strewn all over the floor and counters.

They moved quickly, stepping over discarded pots, pans, and canned goods, en route to the window that needed to be closed in the living room. The volume of the various foreign beasts that lay outside of the building grew as they closed the distance between them and the window. The frigid November air wafted in from the open window, causing a momentary shudder to run through Jeff.

Carl closed the window expeditiously, muffling the unexplainable sounds once again.

The trio stood stone still, listening for any intruders within the apartment, and heard nothing but the clicking of claws patrolling the hallway beyond the front door. Jeff could not be sure based on the variability of the monsters he had witnessed so far, but from the rhythmic clicking, he guessed that there was probably one creature in the hallway within a close vicinity to the group's apartments. He listened closely as the sound faded; the monster moving to the far end of the hallway. *More than likely the one that had grabbed the man we heard try to enter the hallway earlier.* Jeff thought.

Carl observed his wristwatch, registering the time—8:46 in the morning. He relayed the time to the others, his voice strained. "It should be light by now. Whatever's unfolding, this darkness seems like it's here to stay."

Jeff and Kara exchanged glances, a silent understanding passing between them. Kara's voice trembled as she spoke to the escalating madness, "This is utterly insane. Do either of you have any theories on what the hell is happening? I'm grasping at straws, attempting to conjure a rational explanation, but the more we unravel, the more any semblance of real-world reasoning slips away."

An unsettling stillness enveloped the room, shattered only by a deep, guttural roar that reverberated from outside, punctuating Kara's sentence. The sound echoed through the silence, sending shivers down their spines.

Jeff, his gaze fixated on the window, broke the tension. "We can't ignore that. We still need to figure out how to dispose of that creature's corpse from Carl's bed," he stated, his voice a low murmur in the tense atmosphere. "And beyond that, we need a plan. We should try to get to any other survivors before these things do."

The direness of their situation hung heavy as they huddled together, grappling with the unknown. Outside, the darkness seemed to harbor secrets, and the distant roar hinted at dangers yet unseen. As they contemplated their next moves, a newfound determination crept into their collective gaze.

In the faint flashlight beam, the group faced the dilemma of disposing of the dead creature's body that lay on Carl's bed. Jeff ran a hand through his hair, considering their options. "We can't leave

it here, and we can't risk the hall or the window," he said, his voice edged with urgency.

Kara, chimed in, "That thing is in the hall, and outside is crawling with them. We already know most of them have no problem getting in a third-story window. We need a solution that's quick and won't draw attention."

The suggestion of the garbage disposal surfaced, but a collective hesitation filled the room. Jeff voiced the concern shared by all. "It's too loud. We'd be broadcasting our location to anything within earshot. And who knows what kind of pathogens that thing carries? Chopping it up would take hours, exposing us to whatever it's carrying."

Tension hung in the air as they weighed the risks, each option laden with its own peril. In a moment of clarity, Kara spoke up. "Let's throw it out the front door into the hallway. We'll have to deal with that creature sooner or later if we want to reach other survivors. It's a risk, but it's our best shot."

With hesitant nods, the group prepared for the daunting task. As they gathered around the dead creature, Carl voiced what they were all thinking. "This thing smells like absolute garbage, and it can't be rotting already."

A distant shuffling in the hall caught their attention. "It sounds like it's at the other end," Carl whispered, a mix of relief and tension in his voice.

The decision made, they reluctantly grasped the limbs of the creature. Carl taking both arms and Jeff and Kara taking a leg each. They lifted and Jeff grunted, "Damn this thing is solid, it didn't look like it would be this heavy."

"Yeah, try being at this end man," Carl said through gritted teeth, straining with the weight. The group crept the creature towards the door, eyes darting nervously at the entrance. As they reached the threshold, a plan unfolded. "If it gets back here before we can close the door, we need a distraction," Jeff suggested, his mind racing.

Kara nodded; her gaze fixed on the still

closed door. "Let's drop it here before we toss it. We need to get our weapons in case the thing in the hallway is closer than we think. Do you two think you can handle tossing it out if I get the door?" Jeff and Carl nodded, affirming they could. "We can't afford any screwups," Kara finished.

The group's weapons placed within reach, they waited, listening for the hallway beast's footfalls to be on the opposite end of the corridor. Then Kara, hand posted on the handle, asked, "Ready?"

Jeff and Carl responded in tandem, "Ready."

Kara yanked the door open violently. Jeff and Carl, holding the body by the arms and legs, folded as far as the creature's strong spine would allow, heaved the body toward the opening of the front door. Kara, with her knife clutched in one hand, still had her other hand on the door's handle, ready to slam it shut in a hurry.

A distant scramble of claws from the far end of the hallway intensified, drawing perilously closer to the apartment. The creature, seemingly alerted by the creaking door, emitted a high-pitched shriek reminiscent of a fox's hair-raising nighttime cry, amplifying the urgency. The lifeless corpse, propelled by Jeff and Carl's desperate heave, hung suspended in the air, each moment stretching into an eternity.

As Kara attempted to slam the door shut, a macabre twist of fate unfolded. One of the dead creature's arms snagged on the door frame, trapping it in a grotesque limbo between the safety of the apartment and the impending danger of the hallway. Panic surged as the hallway echoed with the clattering of approaching claws.

Carl, positioned closest to the head of the corpse, reacted instinctively, lunging forward to shove the remains out of the doorway. Time seemed to warp as the relentless click clack of claws on the hallway floor intensified, signaling the encroaching threat.

Frantic movements ensued, a symphony of chaos as the survivors fought with the nightmarish intersection of the living and the dead. Each action carried the weight of survival, the boundaries between safety and peril blurred in the desperate struggle against the endless darkness.

In the frantic struggle to repel the growing horror, Carl, fueled by adrenaline and desperation, managed to free the corpse from the doorway. As Kara lunged to slam the door shut, her heart raced with the anxiety of the moment. A long-fingered, taloned hand shot through the narrowing gap, narrowly missing Carl's arm. The group, now united behind the door, heaved in unison a collective effort to defy the inhuman strength of the force outside.

Carl, feeling the weight of impending doom, maintained pressure on the door while stretching his other arm towards his sword, mere inches from his grasp. With each moment, the struggle intensified. A slight release of pressure allowed the door to inch open, permitting more of the creature's long, skinless arm to lash out at the group. The air resonated with the horrifying swishing sound of claws slashing and the group's desperate attempts to hold the door against the onslaught.

As the creature gained ground, its victory at hand, Carl's fingers finally closed around the hilt of the sword. With a swift and determined motion, he brought the blade down hard, severing the creature's arm, a mist of warm liquid painting his face. A sudden, deafening screech echoed through the confined space, and the door slammed shut. The group, momentarily spared from the immediate threat, listened to the creature's anguished retreat down the hallway, its shrieks fading into the distance.

Carl stood frozen, holding the sword in his hand, with the creature's blood dripping from his face. Jeff and Kara panted heavily from the struggle and remained pressed against the door. After a few moments of silence passed between the trio, Jeff spoke, "OK, I know you said not to ask about the sword earlier, but considering it has saved our asses twice now, I gotta know, why do you have a sword?"

Without a word, Carl cracked the door open, tossed the severed arm into the shadowed hallway, and then, with a steadying breath, began to speak. "Growing up, something always drew me to martial arts. My mom raised me and she wouldn't let me sign up for any classes, constantly telling me I would get seriously hurt or paralyzed, like I was some delicate flower or some shit. I secretly started training at a local jiu-jitsu gym. The instructor knew what the deal was at home and let me train for free. He was pretty much my only male role model. When it was time for me to leave for college, my mom moved down south with family. Knowing I probably wasn't coming back, my instructor, gave me this." Carl lifted the sword, its polished blade reflecting the dim light. "When you win big jiu-jitsu tournaments, they give you one of these bad boys. I've had it ever since. Anyway, that's why I have a sword. Now, who wants to help me get this place shored up?"

In the midst of the group barricading the windows and door, Kara picked up Carl's remote and switched on the tv. She was greeted by the "no signal" notification, and as she considered its implications, she inquired, "Do either of you have a radio?"

Jeff held a piece of scrap wood to a window as Carl drilled it in place. "Yeah, I think I have an old one in my bedroom closet if you want to crawl through the wall and get it, it's on the top shelf."

Kara left to retrieve the radio and returned a few minutes later, setting it atop Carl's living room coffee table. She turned the knob activating the radio and spun the tuning dial through the FM range, only receiving static in response.

Carl said, "Try AM, might get one of these local ham radio nuts, but it's better than nothing."

Kara switched and began scanning and fell in on a faint male voice.

"My fellow amateur radio enthusiasts have informed me that this goes as far west as New Mexico, and all the way down to once sunny Florida. I can't say if it goes further than that because my communication chain ends there, but folks this is more than a Montgomery County phenomenon."

CHAPTER FOURTEEN

"Alright, so the beginning of these lines marks where they constructed the ships, and the endpoints are where they ended up. But aside from our craft, none of these destinations correspond to any planets we're familiar with. How is that possible? This thing lacks any visible propulsion system, and even if it did, crossing from one galaxy to another is deemed impossible," Patrick mused aloud to the group.

Crystal responded succinctly, "They're portals."

"Portals, like teleporting?" Scott questioned with disbelief.

"Consider these places as other planets, worlds, dimensions—whatever you prefer. But the starting points on these charts aren't the actual origins. Look," Crystal said, shifting the glass to another starting point. A purple-hued background emerged in the looking glass, revealing five irregularly shaped rock formations, forming a circle in the purple dirt. No crafts or visible scaffolding were present. "They're explorers. They locate these portals on other worlds or alternate realms, venturing from some distant starting point. There's always a circle with five objects surrounding it. Perhaps they begin their journeys from their home world, discovering these unique locations throughout the universe and utilize them to traverse different realms. It seems more reasonable than the idea of the same beings inhabiting hundreds of thousands of planets or planes of existence."

"Or," Patrick interjected, "they aren't explorers at all; they're conquerors, populating hundreds of thousands of other planets."

"Either way, they're not using any means known to man," Crystal concluded, her words hanging in the air, laden with the weight of an enigmatic truth.

During their contemplation, a suggestion bubbled to the surface as Scott broke the contemplative silence. "Crystal, have you tried focusing on the midpoint of one of these lines? It could reveal something more about these mysterious journeys."

Intrigued by the idea, Crystal adjusted the looking glass to hover over the midpoint of a line. As she peered into the glass, a disconcerting void greeted her eyes. No celestial landscapes, no planets, just an abyss of darkness. She moved the glass along the line, yet the emptiness persisted, a stark departure from the vibrant scenes witnessed at the line's endpoints.

Perplexed, Crystal shared her thoughts with the group. "If they were taking pictures along the way why would these lines be blank? Wouldn't you think they would photograph the journey? Why would the entire journey be shrouded in blackness? Unless... They're traveling through a portal."

The group absorbed this revelation, the gravity of the implication sinking in. The looking glass, an artifact of unknown origin, hinted at a method of travel beyond comprehension. Crystal continued her exploration, guiding the glass along other lines, each revealing the same impenetrable darkness. The notion of a portal network connecting disparate points in the universe began to solidify.

"Think about it," Crystal urged, her voice carrying a mix of excitement and trepidation. "If these beings are using portals, it explains the seemingly impossible traversals and the purpose behind these intricate lines on the charts. They aren't merely observing; they're navigating through these portals, leapfrogging across the cosmos."

The room buzzed with a newfound energy as the group wrestled with the significance of Crystal's discovery. The looking glass, an enigmatic conduit, held the key to unlocking the mysteries of the extraterrestrial travels mapped before them.

Crystal continued, "Also, I don't think they're world conquerors. If so, where are the hordes of hostile aliens aboard this craft, and how has it been here so long without making a move?"

Patrick, thinking it over, responded, "Maybe something went wrong with this one. Maybe the crew perished or maybe they've been waiting. Why is it blasting out radiation after lying dormant for so many decades? I'm not sure any of us can answer that."

Kurt cut in. "Speaking of which, finding anything in there about shutting this damn thing down? I'm sure this is all fascinating to ya'll, but if we all disintegrate, what good is it?"

Crystal, ignoring Kurt's comment, turned to the next page in the thick book. On the next page were more of the alien characters indecipherable to the group, but one character amid the scribble was recognizable. "Is that a cross?" Scott asked.

"It sure looks like it, but who knows what it represents to them? It could mean anything," Crystal reasoned, flipping to the next page. The paper unveiled an intricate drawing depicting what seemed to be the construction process of the enigmatic craft. Many components portrayed in the illustration remained unfamiliar to the scientists, though a few, like the peculiar wiring, bore resemblances to human technology. Brief descriptions in the unknown script accompanied various parts, potentially serving as assembly instructions. As the team delved deeper into the manual, the next 50 pages unveiled a more detailed account of the craft's construction.

Among the pages were several compartments that hinted at control rooms, each featuring a complex array of switches and levers. One particular image caught their attention—an uncanny resemblance to the room they currently occupied. In this diagram, the podium they stood before while rifling through the manual was equipped with an array of dials and switches.

The team, now engrossed in decoding the manual's contents, exchanged speculative glances. As they navigated through the intricacies of the guide, each page uncovered more layers of the craft's inner workings. Cryptic notations adorned the margins, hinting at the sophistication of the technology involved. The scientists, captivated by the puzzle laid out before them, began to grasp the depth of knowledge embedded within the manual.

As Crystal turned another page, a section dedicated to the craft's navigation system emerged. Diagrams of celestial charts intertwined with advanced schematics left the team both bewildered and intrigued. It was as if the manual, a key to understanding an alien technology, invited them to decipher its secrets and unlock the mysteries of the cosmos.

Crystal continued to turn the pages, each unveiling an additional layer of the extraterrestrial manual's enigma. The illustrations now included depictions of the completed ship, its sleek design radiating a mystical elegance. One image, however, seized the attention of the group—an illustration that seemed to portray the ship emitting waves of energy, accompanied by the alien writing which, though still indecipherable, now resonated with a more urgent tone. It hinted at a potential purpose beyond mere exploration. The page also contained a drawing of a small pod like structure breaking from the ship.

"That looks a lot like an escape pod to me." Crystal said aloud.

As Crystal delved deeper, the manual unfolded into a section dedicated to a small escape pod-like apparatus. The drawing, though not fully comprehensible, conveyed a sense of urgency and seemed to outline instructions on its utilization. The group stared, absorbing the realization that this manual held not only the blueprint for the craft, but also crucial insights into its functions and potential capabilities.

Turning more pages, the group encountered drawings of alien structures, some distinctly unearthly. Towers and spires reached heights unimaginable, dwarfing anything known to humankind. Other depictions showcased intricate cave systems and dungeon-like rooms, revealing an architectural diversity that defied terrestrial norms.

Then, as Crystal turned another page, an

astonishing revelation confronted the group—
an illustration that captured the construction
of the Egyptian pyramids. The view was aerial,
presenting a perspective not from Earth but from
above, as if observing the ancient construction
from the vantage point of the craft. Tiny figures
toiled beneath hauling massive stones, guided by
colossal beasts unrecognized in human history.

A stunned silence lingered in the room as
the inference of the images sank in. The manual,
a cosmic chronicle, depicted the intervention of
an advanced civilization in shaping the course of
human history. The pyramids, once symbols of
earthly mystery, were now cast in the light of
extraterrestrial influence. The revelation hit the
group like a wave, causing a surge of questions to
emerge as they struggled with the idea that their
craft had shaped the destinies of civilizations on
Earth.

Crystal, her eyes filled with a mixture of
wonder and trepidation, continued to explore
the manual. Every turn of the page unraveled
more intricacies, connecting the threads of
the unknown. The group, on the precipice of
unveiling cosmic truths, braced themselves for
revelations that transcended the limits of human
understanding.

Crystal, her eyes widening with realization,
spoke with a mix of awe and uncertainty.
"So, they've been here before, centuries ago,
influencing ancient history." Another drawing in

the manual emerged, depicting Stonehenge being assembled. This time, however, the colossal rocks were being arranged by giant apes, who were being overseen by hideous horned creatures with whips, an image that further blurred the lines between myth and extraterrestrial intervention.

As the group absorbed this revelation, Scott interjected with a tone of urgency. "Hold on, are we just going to gloss over the part where it shows that if the ship is emitting energy like it currently is, the operator was supposed to get into some sort of pod and travel back through one of these supposed portals to escape!?"

The realization struck like a bolt of lightning, casting a shadow over the room. The manual, a mind-bending tapestry, had illuminated not only the extraterrestrial influence on Earth's ancient civilizations, but also provided a contingency plan for the craft's operators in the face of impending danger.

Crystal, still processing the weight of what they had discovered, responded, "It seems that way. If the ship emits energy like it's doing now, the operator was meant to retreat using some form of escape pod and navigate back through the portals. It's a failsafe, a way to return to the supposed starting point, or perhaps another designated location."

As the room brimmed with a charged atmosphere, the group grappled with the implications of the confusing revelations.

Ancient drawings, the construction of historical landmarks, and the escape protocol hinted at an intricate interplay between alien beings and humankind. The mysteries of the manual wove a narrative that eclipsed time and space, beckoning the team to unravel the secrets embedded within its pages. The urgency in Scott's voice lingered, a reminder that the craft's energy emissions were not just a curiosity but potentially a precursor to a profound event that could reshape the trajectory of their own lives forever...

Kurt, growing impatient with the banter of the scientists, reached out and picked up the book while saying, "Can we take this thing, keep moving, and try to find a damn way to shut this thing down?"

As the book lifted from the podium, an audible click rang out over the humming of the craft. The group froze, looking to where the book had been sitting. They observed the panel displayed in one of the book's diagrams, was sitting beneath the book and its removal had released a turquoise-colored button.

Scott, startled, shouted, "What the hell are you doi—"

The humming grew loud enough to cut him off as two doorways opened on the far side of the chamber, filling the room with a blinding white light.

CHAPTER
FIFTEEN

Ken inched forward within the giant vehicle, the behemoth navigating through a desolate landscape. The twisted wreckage of cars, lifeless corpses, fallen trees, and toppled telephone poles marked the eerie trail he traversed. A silent prayer echoed within him, hoping the absence of people signaled that they had sought refuge, escaping the impending horrors.

The only signs of life revealed themselves in the haunting forms of unearthly creatures. The spotlights, strategically positioned to offer a 360-degree view, cast a disturbing glow on the surroundings. Ken steered the armored vehicle with caution, the occasional glimpse of monstrous shapes in the shadows jarring his nerves. A chilling encounter shook the vehicle when one creature collided with it, producing a hollow gong that resonated through the metal body of the vehicle. Ken stole a glance out the passenger side window, catching sight of a large, hairy entity stumbling away in a drunken stupor.

Despite the fortified cocoon of the vehicle, the darkness seemed impenetrable. Yet, as Ken continued along his path home, he noticed subtle shifts in the shadows. At certain points, the spotlights penetrated deeper, revealing scenes reminiscent of city row homes. However, these city streets, though mirroring the familiar decay, bore the chilling absence of life, replaced by fresh signs of destruction—freshly broken doors and shattered windows.

As Ken traversed the city blocks, the scenes continued to assault his senses. Among the shattered windows and broken doors, corpses littered the streets. Most were unrecognizable piles of meat, missing limbs, heads, and chunks of flesh. The stark brutality painted a gruesome picture of the unfathomable horrors that had befallen this once-familiar urban landscape. There was violence in this area before, but not like this.

The variation in the darkness added an extra layer of disquiet to Ken's already tense situation. Each glimmer of light cast grim shadows that seemed to dance along the edges of the unknown. The cityscape, once a place of familiarity, now held an ominous aura, with the occasional spotlight unveiling fragments of a world consumed by an otherworldly menace.

As Ken continued to navigate through this spectral landscape, the air thickened with an indescribable eeriness. The hum of the armored vehicle resonated like a somber melody, accompanied by the occasional creaks and groans of the desolate surroundings. After he had traversed several miles, he came upon a particular block that seemed unusually quiet, the background noises from mysterious creatures that had been spilling into the night air since the bang all fell silent.

Ken, sensing the stillness, clashed with the feelings of hope that maybe whatever had befallen Philadelphia had begun to abate. Yet a suspicion that something horrible was right around the corner gnawed at him. As he rolled on into the temporarily still night, he saw a recently abandoned gas station a few yards ahead. One pump laid on the ground, knocked off its base, gasoline bubbling up from the hole that lay beneath it. Then he heard a faint cry for help. The voice sounded like a child's and was barely audible over the bumping of the bearcat's tires over the well-worn city streets.

As he neared the gas station, the sound grew slightly louder and clearer, a young child's whimpering.

"Help, help, mommy where are you?"

Ken cracked the window to his vehicle, and the sobbing became clearer. Ken felt the pull to get home, to get to his family, but he couldn't live with himself if he left an innocent child out to be devoured by some monstrosity.

As he turned the wheel to veer toward the

parking lot of the station, he spoke to Loki, "Eyes up boy." The dog perked up from his spot on the back bench seat and jumped to the front of the vehicle, peering out the windows.

As Ken got closer to the spot where the crying was originating from, he saw a small dim light shining through the open doorway of the gas station, the kid's flashlight. *Thank god they're still alive in this,* Ken thought. He parked the vehicle close to the front of the building. The spotlights reflected off the large pane of glass that took up much of the front of the station and its various cigarette ads.

He left the ignition running, looked at Loki and said, "With me boy."

As he stepped out of the vehicle, his boot crunched on something. As he shone his weapon light on the ground, the crunching noise led him to a bone that he couldn't help but suspect was a human femur. Ken held a hand up to Loki, who was in the driver's seat, poised to hop out. Loki, understanding the hand cue, sat and waited.

As Ken extended the beam of his flashlight further into the inky darkness, a chilling discovery awaited him—a littering of bones were strewn about the desolate parking lot of the gas station. The skeletal remains cast spectral shadows, their ghastly presence whispering of unspeakable horrors.

Amidst the skeletal menagerie, a child's voice pierced the silence, emanating from the faint glow of a flashlight. "Is someone there? Please, help me! I can't find my mommy, pleeeeaase."

Ken, his voice cautious yet laced with a semblance of authority, responded, "Hey kid, come to the sound of my voice. I'm a policeman, and you can ride with me and my dog. "We'll get you somewhere safe." The words spoken into a world where safety seemed a preposterous concept.

The child's voice, now trembling and tearful, blubbered back, "But there are monsters out there. Please, help me." The feeble glow from the doorway retreated into the consuming darkness, a few hesitant steps backward.

Ken, uncertainty gnawing at him, took a few steps forward, leaving the vehicle's door ajar for Loki to join him if necessary. From his vantage point by the open driver's door, Loki erupted in a volley of ferocious barks, a visceral response to the encroaching unknown. As Ken approached the opening of the building, a prickling sensation crawled up the back of his neck, the small hairs standing stiffly in warning.

The faint flashlight, a meager companion to the voice, abruptly extinguished. In its stead, a set of haunting, orange-glowing eyes slowly opened, rising to several feet in the air above Ken. The child's voice, once innocent and desperate, warped into a deep, grating tone that cackled maniacally. The grotesque metamorphosis echoed through the shadows, shattering the illusion of rescue and plunging Ken into a realm where the boundary between innocence and malevolence blurred into a nightmare of monstrous proportions.

Ken pointed the shotgun upward toward the glowing eyes and squeezed the trigger, the deafening report temporarily brought ringing to his ears. The eyes vanished momentarily, leaving an unsettling void in the shadows, before reappearing a few feet further away from Ken. As the echoes of the shotgun blast reverberated through the desolate landscape, a chorus of inarticulable whispers emerged, a disconcerting choir that seemed to crawl under his skin. The whispers were more than mere sounds; they were vines of malevolence winding their way into Ken's consciousness, making his head swim with disorientation. It was as if the very air around him was infused with the whispers, insidious words that defied comprehension but carried an undeniable weight of anger. His nose was assaulted with an amalgamation of odors–damp earth, metallic tang, and an underlying scent of decay that clawed at his senses. As Ken slowly backed toward the Bearcat, the whispers intensified, forming a lunatic's orchestra that defied understanding. The bizarre voices seemed to emanate not just from the surroundings, but from the very recesses of his own mind. The glowing eyes, now multiplying in number, appeared not just in front but surrounded him, a nightmarish kaleidoscope of insidious intent.

Ken's heartbeat echoed in synchrony with

the eerie whispers, the rhythm of fear pulsating through his veins. His surroundings blurred as a suffocating darkness closed in. The shotgun felt heavier, as if burdened by the malevolence that now hung thick in the air. Every step backward seemed to plunge him deeper into a realm where reality and nightmare intertwined, and the boundary between the living and the unseen dissolved. The sinister whispers became almost unbearable, seeping into his soul and entwining his very being. He wanted desperately to claw his eardrums out.

Just as the whispering and the glowing eyes reached a crescendo, threatening to engulf Ken in a maddening tapestry of insanity. The ferocious barking of Loki, who was now by his side, emerged as a lifeline cutting through the discord of dread. Each powerful bark served as a beacon, a tether to the real world that provided Ken with both hope and direction. In the relentless onslaught of threatening whispers, Loki's fierce barks became a counterpoint of strength, a tangible connection to sanity.

Loki's frenzy seemed to cut through the veil of mental turbulence, his primal instincts sensing the unseen threats that lurked in the shadows. The dog's fur bristled, muscles tense, and teeth bared in a primal display of protective ferocity. Loki was not just a companion; he was a guardian, a steadfast ally in the face of the encroaching darkness. Ken, now only several yards from the vehicle, turned and ran for the open door. The disjointed whispering intensified and the orange eyes surrounding him seemed to multiply as he flung himself into the Bearcat right beside Loki and slammed the vehicle's door. The whispers turned to a high-pitched shrieking laughter. Ken sped in reverse toward the road. While reversing, he noticed more bones, some of which still wore clothing: a fireman's suit, a catholic school uniform, and a three-piece suit, covering skeletal remains. When Ken was off the lot and back onto the road, the eyes and the laughter faded out like leaving the serviceable range of a radio station on a road trip.

As Ken returned to the main thoroughfare, he reached across the seat and gently stroked Loki's head. The act was a dual purpose–offering solace to the dog amidst the night's trauma and providing a brief respite for Ken himself. A few silent tears traced paths through the grime covering his face, a poignant testament to the emotional toll of the night. As he drove, a brilliant flash bathed the street in an ethereal glow, as if someone had just captured a colossal photograph. Ken's gaze lifted to the heavens, where an ephemeral lightning dance painted the night within the confines of a brooding, obsidian cloud-covered sky.

CHAPTER SIXTEEN

The mysterious voice on the AM radio persisted, a captivating presence that held Jeff and the rest of the crew in a momentary pause from fortifying the apartment. In the stillness, they gathered around, drawn to what they believed to be the final broadcasting voice echoing through the airwaves in the greater Philadelphia area.

The man continued with his Jersey accent, "If youse are somehow listening to this without being holed up somewhere safe, one, thank your lucky stars you're still among the living, and two, get yourself somewhere safe. Preferably a place with no windows and stocked with food and water. We don't know how long this might last, folks. I'm getting reports of all kindsa crazy shit out there and saw a few myself. Some of youse also reported seeing military movement, so hang tight and hopefully our Uncle Sam can whoop some—whatever these damn things are ass."

As the broadcaster's voice continued, Jeff

seized a moment of relative calm to let his gaze wander towards Kara. Enamored with her since the day he first saw her struggling with her mailbox, he remembered the instant connection when he shared the trick of pulling up on the unreliable box's door to open it. Even now, with splatters of an alien creature's blood staining her face and her white AC/DC shirt, Jeff found her remarkably beautiful.

In this brief lull, the bizarre circumstances surrounding them allowed Jeff a moment of reflection. He doubted Kara would notice the disheveled state of his normally pristinely pomaded brown hair, now sticking up at all angles, or that he still wore his plaid pajama bottoms. The rush for survival blotted out all preconceived expectations. The stark brutality of the past several hours had prompted more interaction between them than the entire year she had lived in the same building.

Amidst the chaos and uncertainty, there was a silver lining—a connection forged in the crucible of the bizarre events unfolding. As they navigated the challenges together, Jeff couldn't help but appreciate the subtle beauty that persisted even in the face of the horrors surrounding them. Just as Kara caught Jeff's sidelong stare and gave him a small smile, the amateur radio jockey broke him from his thoughts.

"Speculations ripple through the darkness.

Some say it's the end of days, a hell on earth, or the heralding of an apocalypse. Others argue it's a government project gone awry, or perhaps an alien invasion. Regardless of your belief, one undeniable truth prevails—it's pitch dark at 10:00 AM, and there are undoubtedly man-eating creatures roaming the streets."

The dismaying narrative unfolded further as the unseen speaker shared reports from a fellow enthusiast in Ohio, tales that hinted at spectral-like beings. "Spectral entities," the voice suggested, adding a layer of supernatural mystery to the unfolding chaos. The question lingered, suspended in the airwaves: Was this a celestial reckoning, a precursor to the apocalypse?

The unknown narrator's contemplation turned philosophical as they pondered, "If this is the rapture, it seems the big fella didn't find any of us good enough for a trip upstairs. And if it's a cosmic struggle between good and evil, let me tell you, evil seems to be gaining the upper hand."

In the bleak cadence of the radio broadcast, the mysterious speaker left the group with a chilling admission—an acknowledgment that the forces of evil were prevailing in this nocturnal nightmare.

The trio continued their fortifications while leaving the broadcaster on in the background, hoping for new information that could help them out of their current situation. The hours passed without another violent interaction, but the sounds emanating from the exterior of the building reminded them of the monstrosities that now inhabited the world. Before long, Jeff and the others felt the weariness of the events of the day and lack of sleep weighing on them.

Jeff asked Carl what time it was, and he responded, "4PM. I know, between being woken up ridiculously early, and the nonstop insanity I'm wiped too, I don't know about you two but I'm calling it a night pretty early."

A few hours later, the group deemed the defenses of the apartments adequate. As their collective efforts concluded, they moved to Jeff's living room, where they set up a makeshift sleeping haven. Jeff, dragging his mattress from his room, flipped it to ensure the gore side faced down. Meanwhile, Carl, acknowledging the irreparable contamination on his own mattress from the creatures' blood, resorted to inflating an air mattress. Kara, making do with the circumstances, claimed Jeff's couch as her makeshift bed.

Despite the physical exhaustion, Jeff expected a familiar struggle against sleep. A nightly battle that felt even more daunting given the haunting scenario of abominations wandering the alternate world they found themselves in. The eerie ambiance of their newfound situation only added to the challenge of finding rest. Mysterious creatures continued to call into the night on the outside of the building.

The group, unanimously deciding against taking shifts for sleep, opted for a collective reprieve. There was an unspoken understanding that, if any threat breached their fortifications, the ensuing chaos would promptly rouse them all. As they settled into their unconventional sleeping arrangements, an uneasy tranquility descended upon Jeff's living room, a fragile respite from an unpredictable and nightmarish landscape.

Jeff's mind meandered once more, captivated by the thoughts of Kara. The gravity of their situation served as a reminder that life was precious and fleeting. Determined to seize the moment, Jeff made a silent commitment to himself–if they managed to escape this ordeal alive, he would gather the courage to ask Kara out. In the grand scheme of the horrors they'd faced, the prospect of rejection paled in comparison.

The events of the past day had etched profound realizations into Jeff's consciousness. The sheer fragility of life had become undeniable, emphasizing the importance of embracing every opportunity for connection and joy. To Jeff, the thought of pursuing a romantic connection with Kara held newfound significance, transcending the ordinary concerns of life.

As Jeff contemplated the idea of asking Kara out, he acknowledged that survival had become a powerful motivator. The events unfolding around them had kindled a renewed sense of purpose, a driving force that had been dormant within him for years. The pulse of life now coursed through his veins, urging him to cherish the moments he once took for granted.

In this newfound clarity, Jeff recognized that the worst that could happen, rejection, seemed trivial compared to the resilience he'd discovered within himself. The simple desire to live had become a potent force, propelling him to confront fears and uncertainties that had long held him captive.

Jeff stirred from his slumber, his internal clock estimating several hours had elapsed in the impenetrable darkness that shrouded their existence. The heavy breathing of his companions told him they were asleep. Amidst the deep silence, a subtle disturbance registered in Jeff's consciousness—a faint, almost elusive sound, like a whisper, with a haunting cadence.

Struggling to discern the origin of the sound, Jeff focused on the direction of Carl, who lay on the air mattress. The noise, akin to a muffled squeak, danced in the shadows of the room. Unlike the rhythmic breathing of Carl, this irregular utterance defied explanation, ruling out common nocturnal disturbances. The noise tiptoed in and out of Jeff's awareness, an elusive specter teasing his senses.

In a suspended moment, Jeff held his breath, attuning his senses to the sounds of the night. A fleeting burst of sound punctuated the stillness—squeak, squeak, squeak—before abruptly vanishing. A realization dawned on Jeff, teasing a thought: on this extraordinary night, would he also contend with a surprise mouse infestation? As Jeff strained to figure out that mysterious sound, he noticed something else. It was still abnormally dark, but a faint glimmer of light seemed to sneak into the thick blackness. A flicker of hope sparked in Jeff's mind–maybe, just maybe, this nightmare had an expiration date.

The room, once swallowed by pitch-black obscurity, now played with this strange mix of shadows and a hesitant lightening of the blackness. It was like the darkness was loosening its grip, revealing hints of something beyond the inky void.

This unexpected change threw Jeff into a puzzle. The usual rules of their predicament didn't seem to apply anymore, so his hope was tampered, his expectations, not high but more than before. While reveling in this new discovery, he heard the squeaking again.

"What the…" he muttered to himself, reaching for his flashlight beside him. It still did little to illuminate his surroundings. Out of his peripheral, Jeff thought he saw movement below the sheet covering Carl.

Jeff squinted as he focused on the outline under the sheet. Something seemed off, but the dim lighting and his sleep-deprived mind made it hard to decipher. It didn't appear to be Carl moving, yet uncertainty lingered in the air.

The room, still veiled in shadows, became an insidious playground for Jeff's overwrought imagination. Sleep deprivation casts a distorted lens on reality, and the dim glow barely eased the disquiet.

A flicker of doubt danced in Jeff's mind as he contemplated waking Carl. The outline beneath the sheet resisted easy interpretation, and the room retained a disturbing stillness. Jeff hesitated; his thoughts entangled in the moment's ambiguity.

Ultimately, he dismissed the idea of waking Carl, chalking it up to the tricks his exhausted mind played. The decision, however, couldn't dispel the lingering unease. Jeff shut off the light, enveloping the room once more in absolute darkness. Rolling onto his side, he closed his eyes, preparing for another restless bout with sleep.

Yet, as if mocking his attempt at repose, a single faint squeak pierced the silence. It bored into Jeff's skull, an unyielding reminder of the surreal situation he found himself in. Wrestling with the unsettling notion that madness might have finally caught up with him, he tightened his eyelids, attempting to shut out both the sound and the encroaching doubts about his own sanity. The room, now a battleground between the tangible and the imagined, left Jeff entangled in an additional struggle, unsure of where existence truly lay. Struggling with his sanity and the relentless squeak that continued to periodically remind him of its presence, Jeff succumbed to his exhaustion and drifted back off.

CHAPTER SEVENTEEN

Crystal was momentarily blinded by the light flooding into the room. As she regained her vision, she found she was standing alone in the chamber and that the walls of the chamber were now illuminated with giant screens, reminding her of the drive-in movie she had gone to as a child with her parents, shortly before her father had split town for good. The silent movie projecting on the walls showed a first-person view of the room she was in. The screen shakily moved from the podium she was at to one of the newly opened doorways across the room, the camera operator not running, but moving swiftly all the same.

As the presence gracefully moved through the open doorway, a burst of brilliant light momentarily washed out the screen, unveiling a scene that seemed plucked from the most enchanting dreams. The whiteness dissipated, giving way to a landscape of unparalleled tranquility. Endless hills rolled beneath a bright, clear sky, spattered with a myriad of wildflowers that swayed in a gentle breeze, creating a mesmerizing dance of colors.

People, all clad in the same shade of bright white, dotted the landscape. Their attire varied from shirts and pants to dresses and shorts, but stitched on the front of everyone's top was a familiar symbol, a cross. Faces remained indistinct at a distance, but their shared attire created a harmonious sense against the backdrop of nature's beauty. In the far reaches, a man, flanked by children, one boy, and one girl, joyfully ascended a hillside, their silhouettes painting a picturesque image against the horizon.

Closer to the screen, a woman with long brown hair stood poised, a frisbee in hand, while an eager golden retriever wagged its tail in gleeful excitedness, ready for the anticipated throw. A harmonious gathering unfolded as a group formed a circle, hands clapping and bodies swaying in tandem to the rhythm set by a man playing a guitar at the center.

As the camera approached, revealing the faces in this heavenly portrait, recognition dawned. Patrick, Scott, and Mindy graced one side of a friendly tug of war, their expressions radiant with unbridled joy. On the opposing side, two men and a woman, unfamiliar yet seamlessly woven into the scene, shared in the revelry, each smile a testament to the blissful harmony of this idyllic realm. There in the swaying circle was her mother, who had passed seven years ago. As she looked around the field, she noticed other faces of friends and family, some of which had been gone for years. She observed the movie, perplexed by its meaning and the combination of living and dead.

As she continued to watch the enchanting scene unfold, a subtle shift in the atmosphere occurred. A distant, almost imperceptible blaring wove its way into the idyllic tableau. At first, it manifested as a mere murmur, like the haunting echo of a distant alarm, gradually growing in intensity.

The rolling hills, once a canvas of serenity, seemed to absorb this dissonance. Wildflowers that once danced gracefully now quivered, as if sensing the subtle disturbance that disrupted their harmonious sway. The people in the distance, still engaged in their carefree pursuits, remained oblivious to the encroaching discord.

As the blaring persisted, it rippled through the air, creating a subtle undercurrent that contrasted with the tranquil scene. The continuous wail momentarily overshadowed the apparent serene melodies of the guitar-playing man in the circle.

She felt a twinge of unease creeping in, a dissonance mirrored in the now flickering light that painted the landscape. Faces of the familiar figures, once aglow with joy, seemed to flicker in and out of the blissful scene as if caught in the dance between two realms.

The alarm, now more pronounced, carved through the dreamlike atmosphere, its urgency growing. The once pristine azure sky became tinged with a foreboding hue, casting shadows that stretched across the rolling hills. The golden retriever, once eager and animated, now cocked its head, a subtle shift in its demeanor mirroring the growing unrest.

As the blaring intensified, a sense of disquiet settled over the scene, challenging the picturesque harmony with an undeniable tension. The people in the circle, Patrick, Scott, and Mindy included, cast furtive glances toward the origin of the siren, their smiles faltering as a palpable uncertainty unfurled. The once perfect tableau now stood at the precipice of transformation, the distant alarm echoed through Crystal's mind.

An unnatural orange glow started from beyond the far hill and grew with the now droning alarm siren. It was if a great wildfire had started right beyond the rise. The two children who had been accompanying the man over the hill came running down it. Terror painted their faces and blood spattered the boy's shirt, their adult escort nowhere in sight. From the opposite side of the hill, Crystal could see what appeared to be horns beginning to come into view. Suddenly, she was shaking violently with fear.

"Crystal! Snap the fuck out of it." Kurt shouted, shaking her by her shoulders. She was at the precipice of one of the newly opened doors.

"You do not want to go in there, trust me."

In a daze, visions of the serene setting delving into cataclysm still danced in her mind Crystal responded, "Wha, what happened?"

"I haven't a clue. I woke up on the floor bleeding from my nose, I saw you and Scott shuffling to this doorway, Scott was ahead of you and by the time I got up and tried to stop him he, he like fell through, and then, the screams, I don't know but I've never heard that type of pain before."

Crystal poised at the blinding doorway and screamed into the void, "Scott! Scooooooooott!"

Kurt stopped her with a hand on her shoulder. "I'm telling you I heard the screams. I've been on two tours to the sand, and I've never heard screams like that before. He's gone, I'm sorry."

The contrast of the serene realm fading into chaos left an indelible mark on Crystal's senses. The shift from blissful landscapes to a disconcerting domain shook her to the core. As she glanced around, the surroundings felt distorted, as if the very fabric of this place was unraveling.

Kurt's narrative, punctuated by his own concern, only added to the confusion. The inexplicable occurrence of Scott's descent through the doorway and the ensuing cries of agony, coupled with the absence of Patrick, gave Crystal a feeling of hopelessness. Crystal, still unable to shake off the sensation that they were caught in a surreal vortex, where the boundaries between dream and nightmare blurred.

Unanswered questions hung heavily in the air, mingling with the echoes of Scott's screams. The craft's mystery continued to thicken, and now she was the lone scientist accounted for on the inside. The thought reminded her that Mindy was on the command post outside and should have video of what had happened. However, her attempts to reach out to Mindy were met with silence.

"What did you see when you were out after the flash?" Crystal asked Kurt.

Kurt shook his head, trying to make sense of the bewildering events. "Nothing. I was just out, and the next thing you know, I'm waking up on the floor, chasing after you and Scott."

Concern crossed Crystal's face as she probed, "Did you see Patrick when you woke up?"

"No, just you and Scott doing your weird sleepwalking shit."

Crystal hesitated, her mind filled with vivid images that played on repeat like a movie reel. "I saw something, like a dream, but it felt so real. There were people, like, it looked like heaven, Kurt. They all had crosses on their clothes, and then it all went haywire, and you were shaking me awake. Why the religious thing? We're on a spaceship; it doesn't make sense. Maybe when I saw that thing in the book that looked like a cross, it subconsciously sank in, and then in my dream, it tied in. I don't know," she blurted out breathlessly.

Kurt leaned against a nearby wall, holding his head, contemplating her words. "I don't know. Your theory is that these things travel all over the universe to other worlds or realms or whatever, through portals, right? Well, couldn't our idea of hell and heaven just be an alternate reality you could get to from one of these portals? I mean, it sounds crazy, but look at where we are right now."

As they delved deeper into the conversation, the lines between truth and speculation became nebulous. The notion of portals leading to other realms, possibly even heaven and hell, took root in their minds. The disquiet of their surroundings added a profound weight to the already perplexing discussion.

Kurt and Crystal made their way back to the podium. Crystal attempted to push the button that was released by the book back in, to no avail. "What do we do now?" Kurt inquired.

"Well, we can't go through that door," Crystal said, pointing to the doorway that Scott had fallen into. "What about the other one?"

Kurt hesitantly spoke. "I'm not sure if I want to open any new doors in this place. I'm telling you, you didn't hear Scott. I did. My vote is we try to get out the way we came in, regroup with the folks on the outside and think up another plan. There's nothing in here we've found that can shut this down."

"What about Patrick?" Crystal asked. "We

can't just leave him in here."

Kurt looking around furtively responded "Well he isn't in this chamber so he either went back the way we came, or the way Scott did before I woke up, and again I ain't going in either of those doors that just opened, so that leaves going out the way we came."

Crystal furrowed her brow, torn between the desire for answers and the looming threat. "I get you're spooked Kurt, but going back might mean my friends die. Plus, we would be missing a chance to understand this place, to figure out how to stop it. We owe it to ourselves and everyone out there to explore."

Kurt sighed, running a hand along his suit's helmet. "I can't shake the feeling that this place is toying with us, leading us on some twisted mission. What if it's just a trap, and we're walking right into it?"

"I don't think we can fully understand without exploring further," Crystal replied. "And what about Patrick? We can't just abandon him. He might be on the other side of that door, waiting for help."

Kurt hesitated, glancing around the chamber as if seeking guidance from the mysterious surroundings. "Okay, let's say we go on, but we stick together, no matter what. If things get too weird, we turn back. Deal?"

Crystal nodded, relieved to have reached an agreement. "Deal. Now let's find Patrick and make sense of all this."

As they approached the doorway, unease hung in the air like a plume of smoke. The hum grew more pronounced, and the light beyond the door seemed to flicker with promises and secrets waiting to be unveiled. The decision to move forward weighed on them, a collective breath held as they stood at the threshold of the opening.

CHAPTER EIGHTEEN

Ken, his hands still shaking from the trauma of his most recent encounter, meandered the heavy vehicle around another junkyard of unmanned vehicles. One SUV had visible slash marks running through the front door. Something had torn through the metal body like a piece of parchment paper. The ominous, intermittent lightning assisted in his navigation, but did little to reassure him of an end to the madness. Brief snapshots of the scenes of carnage and freakish abominations roaming the streets chilled him. The lightning, much like the rest of the new world, was abnormal, coming every 20 minutes just to highlight the horrors otherwise hidden by the impenetrable darkness.

As he approached where he judged the on-ramp to the highway to be, the ground trembled beneath the vehicle. A sound like that of a train rolling along its tracks preceded the shaking. Suddenly, lights appeared in the distance much further away than he had spotted anything since the darkness had started. Before he could make out exactly what was heading his way, an enormous boom followed by a giant orange flash illuminated the air, revealing the large protruding barrel of an Abrams' tank.

"Shit," he yelled, pulling hard on the wheel, thinking that the tank operator was firing towards the Bearcat.

His vehicle jumped the curb with a thud. As the tank continued in his direction, another resounding boom echoed through the night. Ken, noticing that the tank was firing behind him, looked to his rear-view mirror. This time the projectile met its mark and momentarily outlined the silhouette of a colossus moving shape right where his vehicle had been the moment before. A skin crawling roar now joined the countless sounds blaring around him. Loki joined the chorus by barking feverishly. As the tank let off another explosion of immense magnitude, the giant silhouetted creature appeared further away, as if it were fleeing the onslaught. To Ken, the creature looked like the skeleton that his high school biology teacher had kept in the classroom, only it was about three stories high and jet black. The tank rolled by Ken, and was followed by three more in pursuit of the creature.

As Ken observed the unfolding pursuit, a convoy of army personnel carriers flew past him, trailing the tanks. Following closely was an armored Humvee, which came to a halt beside his vehicle. A stern-faced man in combat fatigues motioned for Ken to roll down his window. Ken complied.

"Officer, you've got one hell of a set of balls to be out in this shitstorm, even in that soda can. I'd advise you to find somewhere fortified and hunker down until we sort this out. Now, where the hell are you going in this?" the man gruffly asked.

"I'm trying to get home to my family, sir. Have you and your company been west up the expressway at all?" Ken inquired.

"Came from that way, but only as far as West Chester. But I can tell you this shit goes way beyond that. We got reports; it's nationwide, maybe even worldwide. Hard to tell with most communication channels down. We got mobilized shortly after all the lights went out. These things are all over the place, and they come in all varieties. They'll all kill you, but the big ones will peel the top of your Bearcat there like a tuna can. We also got some reports of demon-like specters, craziness, but I ain't seen nothing like that. Charlie here," the man pointed to the soldier next to him, "has a cousin who claims half a company was wiped out in Delaware by some glowing-eyed spirit shit, said they couldn't hurt it with any bullet. I don't know what in god's name is going on here, but I couldn't rule out this being the end of days, son. Anyway, keep your head on a swivel, try not to get yourself killed, and most of all, pray son," the commander said, rolling up his window and following the other vehicles.

Ken watched the convoy recede into the darkness and began to drive again. The night seemed to pulse with a negative energy as Ken navigated through the wreckage, his senses heightened by the eerie glow of the lightning, revealing the monstrous aftermath of an unseen battle. The road ahead beckoned, a perilous trek into the mouth of the abyss of hell.

As he neared the highway, the skeletal remains of more cars and the eerily torn asphalt painted a grim picture. Shadows danced menacingly, and Ken's pulse quickened. On top of the overpass bridge, silhouettes of hideous creatures perched atop abandoned vehicles came into focus, their horrendous forms outlined against the dimly lit sky. As he made his way onto the on-ramp, the lights of the Bearcat illuminated the green I-76 sign. He mused to Loki, "Let's hope traffic is a little less horrible on 76 when the world's coming to an end."

The traffic, as it turned out, offered no respite. Instead of the typical stop-and-go scenario with red brake lights, Ken found himself navigating through a harrowing landscape of driverless, gore-smeared vehicles that were once the vessels of the living. The Bearcat's push bumper became a necessary tool, scraping and shoving its way through tight spots, the metal-on-metal screeching temporarily drowning out the sounds of the creatures in the night. Illuminated by the vehicle's lights, Ken caught fleeting glimpses of creatures, their faces momentarily revealed before they melted back into the shadows. Fortunately, most were human-sized and hadn't dared to challenge the formidable vehicle.

After painstakingly traversing a few agonizingly slow miles, Ken's keen eyes spotted an exit ramp promising a less-traveled back route. Desperation fueled his decision as he veered onto the ramp, hoping that it couldn't possibly be slower than the abandoned and obstacle-laden highway. However, his optimism was short-lived as he encountered a jackknifed tractor-trailer at the bottom of the ramp, forcing him to ease onto the brakes and assess the situation.

The twisted metal behemoth blocked his path, a testament to the havoc that had unfolded. Ken weighed his options, contemplating whether to navigate the maze of wreckage or seek an alternative route. His mind struggled to make a decision in its frantic state, the urgency to make it home clouded his thoughts. He scanned the darkened surroundings, acutely aware that every choice carried unforeseen consequences.

Beside the cab of the wrecked semi, Ken locked onto a narrow opening. The potential path forward seemed like a lifeline, but it would be a precarious fit for the Bearcat. Doubts gnawed at him, questioning whether the vehicle could withstand the force needed to push through if it became wedged. The urgency of reaching home intensified, the weight of time pressed on him. How long had it been since the world plunged into darkness? Almost a full day? And he was still miles away from his family.

Despite the weight of the decision, he pushed down on the throttle with determination. The engine roared in response, the Bearcat hurtling towards the narrow gap. Every second ticked like an eternity, the exigency burned in his conscience like a relentless flame. As they approached the opening, Ken reached across the seat, extending an arm in front of Loki, a silent reassurance to brace for impact.

"Hang on, buddy," Ken uttered, his voice swallowed by the looming tension. The Bearcat collided with the guardrail and semi simultaneously. Their world inside the cab became a band of metallic shrieks. The vehicle lurched, slowing to a crawl, and for a harrowing moment, it teetered on the edge of becoming lodged. The smell of burning rubber wafted through the air as the tires fought against the tension, struggling for every inch of progress.

Ken's heart pounded, the deafening sounds of the struggle filled the cabin. Time hung suspended, each moment stretched to its limit, as the large vehicle fought against the unforgiving constraints of the narrow passage. The darkness outside seemed to close in, amplifying the anxiety within the confined space of the vehicle, a tangible manifestation of the unforgiving travels to home.

Finally, blessedly, with a massive jolt, the bear broke free of the tangled metal and shot out the other side of the wreckage. Ken looked to the side of the semi and saw a human arm still attached to the handle of the driver's side door, as if someone had started to paint it there and the artist was cut short. Connective tissue hung limply where a man should have been attached at the shoulder. He couldn't help but notice the single police patch on the sleeve of the solitary limb. Ken silently shook his head at the sight.

Beyond the semi-truck, Ken found himself traversing the suburbs. Though the streets were less crowded, the atmosphere was unchanged. Abandoned cars and errant bodies dotted the snapshots provided by the lightning and his headlights. Perched precariously atop two large branches of a massive oak tree was a compact sedan. Something had ripped the roof off, making an impromptu convertible of the vehicle. The homes that Ken could see varied from untouched to entire front doors missing, and windows smashed out. Clothing littered some of the well cared for front yards.

A short while later, Ken noticed the acrid smell of smoke permeating the cab of the vehicle. A few fluttering embers gently landed on the vehicle before being extinguished. The smell became stronger as he progressed along the suburban street. Gasping, he watched as the alien lightning briefly lit up his surroundings once more. Where Ken once knew there to be a sprawling development lay a charred, still smoldering wasteland. The rubble of where structures once stood sat in small bonfires throughout the desolate landscape.

The skeletal remains of burned-out vehicles, some still sitting on concrete driveways that appeared to be placed errantly by some mad architect, steamed in the dim light that the lightning provided. Ashes, many still glowing orange snowed on the vehicle now, and a combination of burning wood and plastic assaulted Ken's nose. Turning the wipers on in the beast, Ken tried the radio. He scanned the FM bandwidth and found it filled with static. Switching to AM, he was halfway through the range when a voice broke the static.

"Whether it be some malicious cosmic visitor, a government experiment gone awry, or the biblical apocalypse we are currently facing, one thing is for sure: it is hell on earth out there right now. Uncle Sam discovered that my little operation was one of the few remaining functioning communication methods and paid a visit to my front door a few minutes ago. They wanted me to share this tidbit with anyone alive and listening. Ahem, all residents are advised to shelter in place, barricade windows and doors with anything readily available. Do not, in any circumstance, leave the safety of your home or shelter. When it is deemed safe for the public to leave shelter, they will follow with another message. If communications are restored by that point, they will send the information through all major media. If not, then viewers, you are to stay listening to yours truly. Back to our philosophical discussion, I personally was leaning toward alien invasion early on, but more of the reports that continue to come from some of my affiliates point out that along with the crazy creatures tearing everything up, specters have been spotted, and usually with a gruesome ending for most of the folks encountering them. So, folks, I think we may have a good old fashion judgment day on our hands here. I have full faith in the fine men and women of our armed forces, but if this is biblical, we may want to hold our loved ones especially close."

In the confines of the vehicle's cab, the radio broadcast became a lifeline to information, a tether to a world unraveling beyond the vehicle's armored exterior. Ken listened intently, contemplating the dual nature of his circumstances: the armored vehicle that sheltered him and the nightmarish world beyond its confines. The journey home was no longer just a physical odyssey; it was a psychological tightrope walk between the familiar and the unknown.

CHAPTER NINETEEN

When Jeff awoke once more, a sudden flash of lightning pierced the oppressive darkness, revealing fragments of the room through the makeshift board covering the living room window. The ethereal glow outlined Kara's form on the couch and highlighted the chaotic transformation of Jeff's once-familiar living space. A spark of hope flickered within him; the lightning served as a potential harbinger of change in their world of absolute darkness.

With cautious optimism, Jeff dared to believe that this sudden illumination might signify the end of their predominant nightmare. Yet, as he gazed at Kara and the surrounding disarray, a lingering unease crept into his thoughts —an inkling that this glimmer of light could be just another layer to the gruesome puzzle that enveloped their existence.

Compelled by this mix of optimism and apprehension, Jeff stood and made his way slowly to the porthole covering the window. His eyes fixated on the outside, yearning for the next flash of lightning to pierce the mysterious veil that cloaked their surroundings. The room held its breath, and Jeff's heartbeat synchronized with the rhythmic anticipation of the storm outside.

As he peered into the fleeting brightness brought by the next lightning strike, Jeff's imagination painted vivid but elusive images of the world beyond. Shadows danced erratically, revealing tantalizing glimpses of the outside world. The room transformed into an evasive canvas, each flash a brief respite from the consuming darkness, offering fleeting insights into their surroundings.

In the distance, lightning silently lit up the sky, creating an eerie spectacle. Dark clouds, thick and foreboding, dominated the heavens. No visible tendrils of lightning streaked across the endless dark horizon, just a brooding expanse of clouds that intermittently flashed with a muted intensity. The electric energy in the atmosphere deepened Jeff's feeling of isolation.

Jeff's emotions were divided—the hope of an end to the terror conflicted with the lingering fear that the intermittent light only made their predicament more mysterious. The lightning became a capricious ally, both revealing and concealing, and with each electrifying burst, Jeff grappled with the uncertainty of what lay beyond their obscured sanctuary. The room held its secrets, and the storm outside whispered promises of revelation and potential worsening, weaving a suspenseful dance between anticipation and trepidation.

The lightning strikes persisted, their irregular rhythm extending over five minutes by Jeff's estimate. Each flash offered a snapshot of the outside world, casting an ominous atmosphere over the complex's parking lot. Twisted metal fragments, remnants of cars, and tattered, dark-stained shreds of clothing littered the once familiar space.

Jeff's attention shifted to the edge of the lot, where the tree line concealed and revealed shadows moving with calculated deliberation. The intermittent lightning flashes provided fleeting glimpses, offering just enough visibility to heighten the sense of foreboding. In the next burst of light, Jeff discerned colossal, misshapen forms in the sky. Their silhouettes resembled gargoyles against the stormy backdrop.

The air crackled with an unsettling energy, stealing the air from Jeff's lungs. The malformed shapes, with wings stretched like grotesque sentinels, added a layer of surreal horror to the scene. It seemed as though the storm itself had birthed these horrendous creatures, turning the darkened night into a chilling spectacle that defied the known laws of the physical world.

Jeff's gaze remained fixed on these monstrous figures as he grappled with the disturbing reality before him. The unpredictable cadence of the lightning strikes heightened the anticipation, each prolonged pause deepening the mysterious aura that enshrouded the complex.

At the next flash Jeff looked about the room in more detail, and in its glow he noticed something odd. Was Carl still on the air mattress or had that been just a pillow and the lump of a blanket? Another flash and he knew Carl was, in fact, not in the bed. Using his flashlight, he dashed to the other rooms, the bathroom, kitchen, and Carl's apartment next door, all empty. After exhausting all possible locations, he shook Kara awake.

"Kara, wake up. Carl's gone," Jeff urgently called out, his voice cutting through the hazy atmosphere of the room.

Kara's drowsy eyelids slowly opened, meeting Jeff's anxious gaze. He repeated himself, and her eyes widened with the sudden realization of his words. Sitting up abruptly, she demanded, "What do you mean he's gone? Where the hell could he have gone?"

"I don't know, but I've searched every room of both apartments, and he's nowhere to be found," Jeff responded, a tinge of worry evident in his voice.

Together, their eyes fell upon Carl's air mattress. Beside it lay his sword, a silent testament to his absence.

"I don't think he would have left here

without that," Kara pointed out, her concern mirroring Jeff's.

Pulling the cover from the mattress, they were met with a chilling sight. Dark stains marred the fabric, stains that could only be one thing in this twisted alternate plane. They had let their guards down and thought that because of their fortifications, the room was a sanctuary from the horrors roaming outside. But now, looking at the stained sheets, they knew how feeble their attempts had been.

As the truth hung heavy in the air, Jeff and Kara exchanged a glance filled with unspoken fears. The missing presence of Carl and the dark stains on the air mattress painted a picture of a world slipping further into a cataclysmic abyss. The air in the room seemed to thicken with trepidation. Each passing moment deepened the morbid realization that their world, already fraying at the edges, was hurtling ever downward in a perilous race to death.

Perplexed and unsettled by Carl's mysterious disappearance, Jeff and Kara surveyed their surroundings. The fortifications that once seemed impenetrable appeared intact, leaving them struggling with the question of how Carl could have vanished without a trace.

"Where could he have gone? Everything looks normal, aside from the bloodstains on the covers," Kara murmured. She scanned the room as if searching for hidden answers.

Jeff shook his head, equally perplexed. "I have no idea. I checked every nook and cranny, and there's no sign of a struggle or anything. It's like he just... vanished."

As they pondered the inexplicable situation, Jeff recalled an odd detail. "I woke up earlier to this weird squeaking sound, but I thought it was just my mind playing tricks on me. Carl was still in his air mattress then."

A moment of shared bewilderment passed between them until, almost in response to Jeff's words, a faint squeak echoed in the room. They exchanged glances filled with both trepidation and curiosity.

"What the hell was that?" Kara whispered. Her voice was barely audible.

Jeff's eyes widened as the realization dawned. "That sound... It's the same one I heard earlier. I thought I was imagining things, but now..."

Their eyes darted around the room, searching for the cause of the mysterious noise. The air mattress, the epicenter of their growing unease, offered no immediate answers.

As they listened intently, the squeaking persisted, a wheel in need of oil in the otherwise silent room. It echoed through their beings, a haunting reminder that their perceived haven was not as secure as it seemed.

A shared sense of urgency enveloped Jeff and Kara as they traced the sound. It seemed to shift, elusive and unpredictable, leading them away from the air mattress. The room transformed into a funhouse of shadows, the suspense escalating with each step.

The squeaking persisted, growing in intensity. They knew the source wasn't a figment of their imagination; it was a living presence, concealed in the darkness.

The room seemed to close in around them, and the anticipation of what lurked in the recesses of the apartment intensified, creating a morbid atmosphere that hinted at the revelations yet to come.

As Jeff and Kara followed the source of the squeaking sound, it led them into Jeff's bathroom. He couldn't shake the feeling that they were on the verge of a horrible discovery, though the anxiety lingered.

"I already checked in here, and Carl wasn't around," Jeff insisted, his brow furrowed with a mix of confusion and concern.

But as they scanned the room anew, they noticed peculiar details missed in the previous sweep. Upon closer inspection, the ceiling vent bore disturbing stains that dropped to the floor, a silent marker of something awry. Jeff, hesitant yet compelled, approached the vent. Hanging delicately from the vent was a small, beautiful purple flower. As he approached, it let out a small squeak. As he got closer and reached toward the flower, the flower retracted into the vent grating;

the vent sprung open, and a hideous purple tentacle emerged. Jeff observed in horror that small teeth ringed the suction like cups on the tentacle.

Jeff's body went rigid with terror as the tentacle, almost like that of an octopus, shot out for him. He stumbled backward, falling to the floor as the tentacle stretched further for him. Kara, quick to react, grabbed a shampoo bottle from the shower and hurled it at the intruding appendage.

The tentacle wrapped around the bottle and emitted a final squeak. With a sudden and unexpected force, it retracted, disappearing up into the ceiling vent taking the bottle with it. The bathroom returned to an eerie quiet, the echoes of their discovery hanging in the air.

Jeff, recovering from the shock, clung to the edge of the bathroom sink, his breaths shaky. Kara, equally unnerved, stood by his side, shuddering, their eyes fixed on the vent as if waiting for some explanation.

The atmosphere seemed charged with mourning, an unspoken understanding settling between them. Carl's disappearance had taken an unexpected turn, revealing a nightmarish reality. These things could get them from anywhere. The bathroom, now tainted with the presence of a single translucent purple tentacle, left them with more questions than answers, but reminded them they were not safe, not here or anywhere.

Kara sobbed softly, questioning the

possibility of it all. Jeff, his head shaking slowly, fought with the weight of Carl's loss. Though their time together was brief, the ache in his soul lingered, a poignant reminder of a connection severed too soon.

The morbid epiphany momentarily overshadowed Jeff's sorrow, fueling his anger at their situation. The world had descended into chaos, and despite their tireless efforts—killing one of these creatures, fortifying the place like Fort Knox—a damn tentacle sneaks through the vent and does what?! Forces Carl through an opening barely large enough for a man's head. Jeff's anxiety increased as he contemplated Carl's strength and confidence; *if Carl couldn't survive, how could Jeff possibly protect them?*

Once Jeff's frustration settled, he turned to Kara with a straightforward plan. "Alright, here's what I'm thinking. We're going to have to take turns sleeping now, keep an eye out, and if you've got any ideas for dealing with bathroom breaks without being sucked down the drain, please let me know. Also, what do you think about leaving a message on the windows? If the military or authorities happen to drive by, it could be our only ticket out."

Kara, still sobbing, nodded in agreement. They then morosely wandered from the bathroom, butting a chair under the handle of the door, and began searching for something to write their message with.

CHAPTER TWENTY

Kurt was the first to breach the threshold, closely followed by Crystal. The bright glow that was coming from the doorway seemed to shut off as they entered what did not appear to be another chamber but a subterranean landscape. The smell of sulfur wafted into their faces as they stood just inside the doorway. "What the hell is going on?" Kurt exclaimed.

Turning around to look back in the chamber they had come from, Crystal gasped. "It's gone, the doorway it's not there!"

Kurt turned, his jaw dropping. "I guess I shouldn't be surprised at this point. Nothing makes sense here. I can't make up from down. Well looks like going back isn't an option anymore."

Black, glistening stalagmites protruded from the ground, their sharp angles creating a menacing forest within the cave. Overhead, the very tips of stalactites hung menacingly, vanishing into the darkness of the vast cavern. An unnatural heat enveloped Kurt and Crystal as they ventured deeper, akin to walking into a scorching oven. Heavy humidity clung to the air, causing sweat to pool on Kurt's forehead, while Crystal's face mask began to fog up, obscuring her vision.

Amidst the oppressive heat, a strange chittering interspersed with humanesque anguished moaning echoed from the unseen depths of the cave system, sending shivers down their spines. The pair, now further regretting their decision, felt a compiling sense of unease in the shadowy abyss.

"Dammit, I knew we should have turned back when we had the chance!" Kurt exclaimed; worry etched across his face. He peered ahead into the dank cave system, where an ominous atmosphere seemed to thicken.

Crystal, trying to maintain composure, responded, "Are you religious?"

"Loosely. I don't go to church or anything, but I was raised Christian, and I believe. However, I don't think we should jump to any conclusions here; it's an alien ship."

Kurt, his gaze fixated on the cavern's depths, couldn't shake a growing sense of dread. "Cosmic powers over this present darkness... spiritual forces of evil in the heavenly places," he quoted, recalling Ephesians from the Bible. He gestured towards the foreboding expanse of the cave system. "Maybe the two could be interconnected?" As he spoke, the narrow path ahead seemed to wind deeper into the darkness, the faint orange glow of magma tendrils now visible, casting sinister shadows that flowed along the walls. The sounds intensified, creating a disturbing harmony with the threatening surroundings. Kurt continued, "I haven't kept up with organized religion either, but my mom had us at church every Sunday growing up, when I left for the army I kind of fell out of going, but a lot of it stuck, maybe we are being punished, maybe this is all part of God's plan or the start of the end of days." His words resonated within Crystal as they kept moving forward, occasionally shouting Patrick's name, hoping he might be in one piece somewhere amidst the harsh rock.

The walls skittered with the movement of creatures concealed within the darkness of the cave system. The feeling of being watched and followed made Crystal's skin crawl. She had thought on a few occasions she had viewed glowing eyes in the periphery of her vision just to find them gone when she turned her head to face the source.

"Watch your step," Kurt shouted as Crystal stutter-stepped, realizing she was about to step on something, a smooth black shape that blended in with the dark ground of the path.

"What is it?" Crystal asked, no one in particular. Then the smooth black rope tensed, stringy muscles contracted under the smooth scaled skin.

"A snake? In here, must be a big one," Kurt said, gesturing toward the tail of the serpent that laid in the path. Stepping over the writhing muscular rope, he shined his light into the darkness at the edge of the path.

The snake's body was larger and thicker than any python Crystal had known to exist. It ran on into the darkness. Something was not quite right toward the other end of the snake, which faced away from them, disappearing into the darkness. As the creature turned to face the source of the light, Crystal found her gut curdle at the repugnant visage staring back at them.

Affixed to the giant body of the snake looking back at them was the head of an elderly man. White pupil-less eyes stared blankly at them. Equally white hair sat atop the head and the toothless mouth contained graying gums visible in the faint light. The white, dead eyes fixed on them, the creature made a wet retching sound as its jaw unhinged, opening wider than the normal rules of anatomy should allow. As the jaw opened wider, a large dripping shape began to slowly emerge from the mouth. As the nauseating retching sound continued, the beast regurgitated a limbless torso; it hit the ground with a moist splatter. Brown foul smelling liquid dripped from the creature's mouth. It emitted an agonizing soft moan, slowly turned and slinked off into the darkness, leaving the pile of gore in view of the duo. There was movement from the shadows.

Bloated, foot long worms wriggled from the dark and climbed atop the pile of decaying flesh, soft suckling sounds emitted from the nauseating scene.

Crystal's hands expeditiously reached to remove her helmet. Moments after she removed it, she vomited onto the dark ground. More of the hideous worms came to the pile of partially digested food. Crystal furiously began stomping on the vile worms, wet popping sounds interrupted by her inarticulable grunting. She slowly turned to Kurt, a string of clear saliva dripping from her mouth. "I'm so sorry. We shouldn't have gone through that doorway. I should've listened to you."

Kurt, visibly shaken, attempted to blink away the horror that had just unfolded. "We couldn't have known this; it isn't your fault. Extraterrestrial involvement or not, this is hell, or at least our interpretation of it. Based on that book, they were here a long time ago. Maybe ancient people have witnessed this. Maybe this is where the idea of hell from the bible originated," he murmured, his voice trailing off.

With no other choice, the two continued down the narrowly lit path, the orange glow of magma running aside the path providing a dimly lit orange hue. The movements within the shadows of the walls and darkened area behind the trail continued along with the dreadful sounds echoing through the cavern. Crystal still caught fleeting glimpses of eyes glowing in the darkness.

"How long have we been in this thing?" Kurt asked as they walked.

Glancing at her watch, Crystal answered, "Three hours since we made the initial entry to the craft, but who knows what that moment was in the outside world? I don't think the laws of time apply in here."

Kurt's brow furrowed in a mix of exhaustion and unease. "It feels like an eternity. Everything's so fucking disorienting."

Just as he finished speaking, a distant groan echoed through the shaft, an inexplicable mix of whispers accompanying it. Crystal's eyes widened, and she instinctively interrupted Kurt. "Did you hear that?"

Kurt halted mid-sentence; his senses heightened. "Hear what?"

A whimpering, unmistakably human, floated from the depths of the cavern. It cut through the ambient moans. The sound was hauntingly real, a stark contrast to the strange noises that surrounded them.

Their footsteps became hesitant as they moved toward the source of the whimpering. The black walls seemed to absorb their every sound, creating a surreal atmosphere. "Is someone else in here?" Kurt asked, his voice carried a mixture of concern and disbelief.

Crystal, her hand gripping her flashlight tighter, nodded. "It sounds like a person, not like those other noises. Patrick! Is that you?"

They navigated the labyrinthine passages, each twist and turn unveiling new rock formations jutting at odd angles. The whimpering grew louder, and as they approached a junction, the source became clearer. They discovered a figure stuck in the middle of the path. From afar, it looked as if the man in the suit coat had fallen into a hole within the path and become stuck from the waist down. The man looked up with wide, desperate eyes as the flashlight revealed his tear-streaked face.

Kurt, his initial shock giving way to curiosity, cautiously approached. "Hey, are you okay? How the hell did you get in here?"

The unknown man wore a suit jacket and a hair style that seemed dated. Crystal thought, *he's dressed like a 1950s businessman.* As they closed the distance, they saw a few of the repugnant worm creatures detach from the man's face and crawl into the darkness, revealing ragged sores on the skin beneath.

Then the man's disconcerting response amplified their growing terror. "You shouldn't have come here. There are things—horrible things in here. They'll keep you here forever, feed on you."

Crystal, assuming the man had succumbed to insanity from being stuck in the hellscape for who knows how long, moved to help dislodge him from the hole he had become wedged in. As she approached, she gasped. "Oh my god, Kurt, he's not stuck in a hole."

Kurt approached and felt his head spinning as he witnessed the morbid display. The man's body appeared to be attached to the smooth stone, his torso welded to the surface. A ring of raw flesh surrounded the man's torso as if he was a half-burned candle, his flesh the wax that fused him to the stone. His suit bore holes where more raw flesh peaked through and slimy cord, like mollusks, moved within.

"You could have the spot right next to me if you wanted Crystal," the man spoke, revealing a brown sparsely toothed grin. "Hey soldier," the man continued. "Use that rifle there and put me out of my misery, I don't know if it'll do me any good, but I hear you're pretty good at it, right... Kurt, don't you want to add a few more hash marks to your tally, c'mon easy pickens here, you like the easy shots right soldier man?"

Kurt stood stone still. He was transported back to a different place. Scenes from his horrible tours overseas flashed through his head. So many nights on the wall of the base, so many life-or-death decisions that any soldier had to make in that situation. The split-second decision to kill a person who may try to rush the compound with a bomb. He had witnessed firsthand women used as sick puppets by the enemy to approach a base, pretending to need help from the soldiers and then detonate the hidden explosive, tearing good men to pieces.

Crystal broke him from his waking nightmare and grabbed him by the arm, pulling him past the man down the path. "Don't listen to it. It's trying to mess with your head, the ship, or whatever is in control here is trying to screw with your mind. It's not real, that's not a man."

As she pulled Kurt down the cavern away from the marionette of a man, it mockingly said, "Please, help me, pleeease." It devolved into a spurt of malicious laughter and punctuated it with, "You are already dead, don't you know that? Why do you think you are here, fooooor your sins!"

Kurt confided in Crystal, his tone soft. "I wasn't being honest when I said I hadn't seen anything while I was unconscious. When we were out, I was back in the war, reliving the things that I had done. This disturbing voice was talking to me the whole time, just whispering horrible shit. It kept saying' you're home now Kurt, you're home."

CHAPTER TWENTY-ONE

"Behold, the day of the Lord comes, cruel, with wrath and fierce anger, to make the land a desolation and to destroy its sinners from it."

The AM radio jockey went on quoting bible verses and talking about the end of days. The war between heaven and hell was likely going on right now. Through the smoldering remains of the last neighborhood, Ken pressed on, the wipers incessantly cleared the ash that descended like ghostly snowflakes. The world around him felt increasingly forsaken, the remnants of neighborhoods reduced to charred memories, representative of this new plague scourging the earth. The haunting echoes of the wannabe radio preacher's words lingered, adding a layer of desperation to the already dire atmosphere.

Curiously, Ken noticed a change in the heavens above. The lightning, once sporadic and distant, now pulsed with heightened intensity behind the thick clouds. The intervals between flashes grew shorter. It was as if the very sky bore witness to the turmoil unfolding on Earth, and Ken again found himself torn between explanations for the madness. Had the underworld risen to earth, or had an advanced malevolent visitor decided to wipe out the current global inhabitants?

Navigating further into the suburbs, Ken found himself in a strangely paradoxical situation. The once-familiar neighborhoods, now eerily quiet, revealed fewer of the grotesque creatures that had plagued the city. A strange thought crossed his mind – were these abominations drawn to areas with more people, feasting on the fragments of human existence?

The desolation and the darkening sky intensified Ken's sense of foreboding. Every mile brought him deeper into an unknown realm, where the lines between reality and nightmare melded. The radio jockey's apocalyptic sermon, the relentless fall of ashy residue, and the disconcerting dance of lightning created an atmosphere of impending catastrophe, and above all, he was worried about the fate of his family.

As the suburban neighborhoods gradually yielded to the embrace of forests and cornfields, Ken noticed a shift in the scenery. The traces of once-bustling communities gave way to a more tranquil expanse, and signs of carnage became increasingly scarce. The occasional burnt-out vehicle or lingering dark stain on the road punctuated the serene landscape, but at longer intervals along the scenic roadway Ken now traversed. He did occasionally spot a set of glowing eyes in the woods and shadows moving that he knew not to be the usual deer of the area, bringing back the horrid memory of the gas station.

The transition to the rural countryside, a place he had always cherished for its distance from the chaos of the city, invoked conflicting emotions in Ken. He relished the tranquility and expanses of nature, but now faced with a mysterious calamity, he couldn't help but feel a pang of regret. Sarah had been open to living in the suburbs or even closer to the city, but it had been Ken who insisted on a life in the countryside, where they could spread out and enjoy a slower pace of living.

As the miles passed beneath his wheels, Ken's mind echoed with the what ifs. If only he had acquiesced to Sarah's preference, he might have been closer to home by now, shielding his loved ones from the threat that unfolded. The regret lingered, a bitter companion on his never-ending journey.

The scenic roadway, flanked by thick forests and golden fields of corn, painted a picturesque scene that belied the turmoil of the world beyond. It was a bittersweet reminder of the life he had chosen, now juxtaposed against the urgency to reach his family amid the permanent darkness. The rhythmic hum of the engine underscored his solitude. He eased the vehicle to a crawl, nearing a narrow single-lane concrete bridge stretching over a small creek. Instinctively, he slowed, scanning for any signs of a vehicle approaching from the opposite direction. Recognizing the slim chance of encountering another vehicle, he accelerated again. As he began up the bridge, he slammed on the brakes, narrowly avoiding hurtling into the small ravine as the sight of the collapsed bridge came into view of his headlights.

Crumbled concrete sat in mounds intertwined with a pickup truck who had not been so lucky. The creek water flowed around the wreckage as if it had always been there. Ken muttered, "Damnit, what now boy?" To Loki.

He knew he could not backtrack all the way to the next closest alternative route. It would set him back an hour on a normal day. While he was mulling this over, he spotted a well-worn path cutting off of the side of the bridge into the creek. A footpath probably trampled down by trout fisherman and wildlife. The Bearcat was equipped with four-wheel drive, but the creek bed was rough and involved a steep climb to the other side of the bank. If he somehow became stuck and couldn't use the winch to get the Bearcat free, he could probably walk the last 10 miles or so to his home, he surmised. He shuddered at the thought of walking 10 miles in whatever this was he found himself in.

After a brief pause, with no apparent better alternative, Ken shifted the Bearcat into four-wheel drive and cautiously descended into the creek bed. Despite the vehicle's considerable height, he could see the water creeping perilously close to its baseboards, a silent threat of potential flooding. Navigating the treacherous path, he crawled slowly, allowing the tires to grapple with the slippery rocks beneath. A sudden dip and shudder startled him. "Shit," he muttered, realizing the front tire had plunged into an unseen hole beneath the water.

Ken stomped on the throttle, the engine roaring, but it seemed reluctant. Trying to break free, he reversed the Bearcat and slammed it back into forward, hoping to dislodge the behemoth from its submerged trap—all to no avail. The vehicle remained steadfastly stuck. In the eerie quiet that followed, Ken thought over his predicament, searching for a solution amid the shadows of uncertainty.

Ken glanced at Loki. "Looks like we're getting out to hook up the winch, my friend." Surveying the woods and creek bed, he found no immediate signs of inhuman threats. Taking a deep breath, he cracked open his door, ears attuned to the foreign sounds. Most of the growls seemed distant. Seizing the moment, Ken leaped out of the Bearcat. The frigid water flooded his boots, sending an icy shiver through him. Loki, splashing beside him, followed to the front where Ken began unraveling the winch.

With the winch prepared, Ken scanned the

opposite bank for a sturdy tree. A subtle splash, incongruent with the steady creek flow, caught his attention. Scanning the dark water around the Bearcat, he saw nothing out of the ordinary. The silence held a tinge of unease as he continued his task, wary of the dangers lurking in the shadows.

Ken trudged through the creek, splashing the cold water as he went and climbed the opposing hill when he heard the sound of a soft splash again. This time, Ken could have sworn he glimpsed an out-of-place ripple dancing atop the stream, as if something had just submerged. His mind wandered, recalling a nature show portraying a Nile crocodile stealthily gliding beneath the water's surface, closing in on an unsuspecting wildebeest by the river's edge. The possibilities of what mutant being might lurk beneath the dark surface in this new unfamiliar place made his skin break out in gooseflesh. Urgently, Loki by his side, he secured the steel cable to a robust oak tree, its strength giving him a semblance of reassurance, and began his cautious descent down the hillside, eyes darting warily between the shadows.

Ken withdrew his Glock from its holster and activated the weapon mounted flashlight, scanning the water before walking back into its chilly embrace; he wished he hadn't left the shotgun in the vehicle but had needed his hands to work with the winch. The coast, seemingly clear, he waded back into the creek. Once at the front of the vehicle, he activated the automatic winch, his grip unwavering on the Glock. He and Loki climbed inside the cab and Ken mashed the throttle. The Bearcat lurched forward. "C'mon you bastard!" he shouted as the engine roared and the tires spun, kicking up muddy creek water.

With a sudden jump, the vehicle broke free of its entrapment, and Ken drove it up the opposite hill. He hopped out of the vehicle again with Loki at his side, the pair still leery of any potential ambushes. Ken began to untie the cable from the oak tree and, amidst the trickling of the creek, he heard the splash again. He immediately turned, weapon in hand, searching the inky waters and caught a glimpse of red eyes sitting atop the water, watching them. The eyes blinked and then quickly submerged when the light hit them. Ken threw the cable to the ground and yelled, "C'mon boy." They ran for the driver's side door.

Ken hurriedly jumped into the vehicle, Loki was a black blur, leaping over his lap and dousing him with water. Hastily slamming the door shut, he jammed his foot on the throttle. Glancing at the driver's side mirror, he beheld a smooth, crocodilian shape slowly ascending from the creek, black water cascading down its sizable frame. It was as if the forces at play had conjured up the monster from his thoughts. He blinked and looked again and saw that the shape reflected back at him was now more indiscernible, but the glowing eyes cut sharply through the darkness.

Despite hurtling forward through brush and scraping trees, time seemed to stretch as Ken watched the phantom shape in the mirror, growing larger than logic dictated by something hidden in such a modest creek. His body tensed, teeth grinding together with anticipation as if the vehicle were about to be plucked from the ground, much like a boy might snatch a grasshopper from a weed. Breaking through the tree line onto the road, Ken watched the enormous shape fade into the trees.

Ken reached across the seat, patting Loki's wet head. With a wry smile, he quipped, "You smell like shit buddy." A humor-laden remark, a familiar coping mechanism he, like many seasoned officers accustomed to witnessing horrors daily, used to mask the lingering weight of trauma. Ken would never admit it, but the dog had been better than any departmental mandated therapy for the many traumas throughout his career.

As the headlights continued rolling down the back road, Ken noticed that although the stars and moon were still absent, there seemed to be a mild abatement in the all-encompassing blackness. The lightning's intervals were also increasing in frequency and had taken on a red hue.

In the background, beneath the road noise, the last radio jockey left in the greater Philadelphia area had seemingly made up his mind about the cause of the event as he quoted more biblical verses.

"Hell from beneath is excited about you, to meet you at your coming; It stirs up the dead for you, all the chief ones of the earth; It has raised up from their thrones All the kings of the nations."

CHAPTER TWENTY-TWO

After Jeff and Kara checked the other vents of the apartments for anything suspicious, they fortified them the best that they could with duct tape. They then made a makeshift sign from a bedsheet and quickly and cautiously hung the sign out a window. The sign had the single word "help" written on it with red paint they had found in Carl's apartment. Jeff found himself thinking again of the hopelessness of their situation and losing Carl. He had been steadily building confidence that the three of them had a chance at making it through this strange event. That confidence had crumbled when Carl was taken.

The will to survive still lingered within him, but he found himself revisiting some of the dark thoughts from his lowest moments before the world was turned on its head. These contemplations were always present, more like a lingering whisper. A surrender to life's uncertainties, and at times, a silent hope that perhaps something would release him from the relentless struggle known as life. Kara stood as the last flimsy tape holding together the house of cards that had become his will to go on. Yet, amidst the chaos, he sensed a need to confront these shadows and fortify the fragile structure of resilience that remained.

Kara said, "I know this sucks and I want to grieve this as much as you do, but I think we need to continue with the plan. We should see if anyone else is alive in this place and try to all work together to find help or something."

Jeff responded in a defeated tone, "They can get you from anywhere, even the damn vents. I doubt there is anyone else alive in here. Why haven't we heard anyone else? These things, they probably have gotten them all."

"You don't know that. If they've got half of a brain, they're probably trying to keep quiet, just like we are. Whether or not you want to try, there is strength in numbers. We have to at least try. What else are we going to do, just wait here to die?"

As the remnants of their conversation lingered in the room, Jeff wrestled with the grim predicament, his mind haunted by the monstrosities still lurking in the dark. Kara's determination, however, flickered like a fragile flame in the midst of the darkness. It urged them to muster the strength to face this together. The gravity of their situation demanded a choice–to succumb to despair or to embrace the glimmer of hope that still lingered in the shadows of their besieged sanctuary.

Jeff's mind raced as he considered their situation. The flickering crimson flashes outside seemed to mirror the tumultuous decisions they faced. In a life marked by solitary struggles, the idea of shouldering this level of responsibility for others was uncharted territory. Of course, he had to keep a classroom of kids in line, but this was nothing like that. He hadn't been used to anyone relying on him, but circumstances forced him into an unexpected role.

As he scanned the room, thoughts swirled like storm clouds in his mind. He couldn't shake the irony of the rosy glow; the world outside might be crumbling, but within this room, determination stirred in his core. The weight of responsibility settled on his shoulders, challenging his very nature.

The plan to survive wasn't clear-cut, but he couldn't ignore the call to action. Drawing on reserves he never knew he had, he started to put together an idea. The red flashes outlined a path ahead–uncertain, perilous, yet undeniably alive.

Jeff looked at Kara, a serious expression on his face. "Let's take back the complex."

As Kara responded, Jeff saw her lips moving, but a deep, grating voice that resonated in his bones washed her voice out. "You could try Jeff... but lying down to die is so much easier. It's what you wanted before. Let us make it easy for you.

Come to us Jeff."

CHAPTER TWENTY-THREE

Crystal and Kurt, with no other option, pressed forward in the hellscape. Crystal could not shake the feeling that they were being watched. She could not tell whether it was the creatures slinking in the shadows or some malevolent all-seeing being. She had expected technology beyond that of the human race when working on the project, but not like this. Either an advanced species with the ability to project images and thoughts into their brains, or something darker.

She had always believed in some sort of higher power, but balked at the idea of angels and demons. She supposed that if the life forms had the technology to visit so many distant worlds, that telepathy wasn't too far-fetched. Yet she could not shake the idea of a malicious higher force being a part of this horror. Almost as unsettling was the alternative, a highly sophisticated alien species that was clearly hostile. It was hard to ignore that cross symbol inside the book. The portal locations surrounded by five objects also made her think of a possible demonic connection. Five points, just like a pentagram. It could have been a coincidence, but now she wondered.

Another possibility crossed her mind as they walked on among the moans and cries. What if the ship's architect wasn't malicious, but something had gone wrong, inadvertently causing portals to open to other realms, some of them horrible? Kurt's words about alternate worlds and hell possibly being one of those alternate realms could be plausible. Her thoughts then moved to Kurt. This thing had really gotten to him, his recount of the vision and the man thing had left him visibly disturbed. He hadn't spoken since telling Crystal about the vision and had since worn a pained expression.

Kurt was deeply troubled, a lingering discomfort that refused to dissipate. The visions from their unconscious state haunted him, but he couldn't bring himself to tell Crystal the whole truth. The voice had become a disturbing companion in his mind. When it had started, it was an errant word here or there, barely audible. Kurt had chalked it up to the fact that they were in a cave system with a bunch of freakish monsters. The voice had persisted though, the words, although still a whisper, had become clearer.

It urged him to join them, whatever

"them" meant. The voice grew more insistent, weaving its dark suggestions into his thoughts. The voice slithered through Kurt's consciousness, a nefarious murmur beckoning him toward a sinister choice. "Kill her," it urged, the words resonating in the depths of his mind. "She doesn't care about you. You're just a tool, a blunt force object wielded to further her agenda."

Kurt clenched his jaw, trying to silence the insidious suggestions echoing within him. The internal battle intensified as the voice persistently fed doubts and suspicions into his thoughts, sowing seeds of discord in the fragile alliance that held them together.

Kurt grappled with these intrusive thoughts, fearing that it would wear him down until he did the unspeakable. He glanced at Crystal, unaware of the internal conflict he was facing. The weight of the voice's whispers pressed on him, a heavy burden that threatened to shatter the shred of stability he had left.

As they navigated the unknown terrain, Kurt battled the presence in his mind. The struggle intensified, and he questioned the origin of the dark whispers. Was it an external force or the unraveling threads of his sanity in this twisted reality?

The voice persisted, its deep whispers weaving through the fabric of Kurt's thoughts, a constant reminder of his ever-morphing environment. The unease grew, casting a pall over their journey, and Kurt fought with the silent, internal turmoil threatening to consume him.

As they meandered around an outcrop on the wall, they froze. Lying in the middle of the footpath was a familiar shape, Patrick. He was lying on his back, eyes closed and motionless. As they approached, Crystal turned her head emitting a choked sob. His protective suit was split from chest to groin. Entrails lay strewn about his body in an obscene mess. The repugnant worm creatures crawled from the opening, fleeing into the shadows at Crystal's approach. His left arm had been gnawed to a stub at the shoulder by something large. As Crystal turned away from her friend, fighting off a bout of uncontrollable sobs, Kurt approached the body.

Kurt, not knowing Patrick before this bizarre event, felt apathetic. As he studied the ragged opening of Patrick's abdomen, he nearly jumped when the corpse's eyes opened. Crystal several yards back on the trail, grieving, did not hear the faint yelp that escaped Kurt's lips. The corpse sat up slowly, more entrails falling from the gaping wound. The dead eyes locked on Kurt's and the voice that emitted was not Patrick's. Instead, a voice like that of three people trying to speak at once came from the body. "You know what you must do. If you don't, you both become worm food. Do it and you'll get to leave. You'll get to be one of our soldiers. You've got what it takes. We've seen your handy work." The corpse giggled with this vile fact. "We only choose the best to be a part of our army. Time is running out; you've got to prove yourself Kurt."

"No, I won't do it," Kurt whispered, a weak rebuttal.

"You're both going to die here then, slowly, in the worst way imaginable. You would be showing her mercy to put a bullet in her. Why not join us, live eternally, and give a quick death to her? She'd do it to you, if we gave her the offer. You're more valuable to us though Kurt, so you get the deal."

"I won't do it!"

Crystal was at his side grabbing his arm. "Kurt, who are you talking to? Are you okay? What's wrong?"

Kurt looked at Crystal. "Nothing, I just thought I heard something." Looking back, the body was motionless, still on the path.

Kurt, again, found himself questioning actuality. *Was his mind just breaking?* He had been in plenty of high-stress situations before and had never hallucinated. Maybe it was something in the air inside the ship, or cave, or wherever the hell they were. Crystal clearly had only heard him speaking, not the marionette of Patrick's body. It had been so real, he couldn't have imagined it. But there lay the unmoving corpse of Patrick.

He felt as if the deeper they traversed into the abyss, the stronger the pull of the voice. The more it made its horrible suggestions, the more mind-bending horrors he experienced. Kurt could feel his pulse quickening with every step. His mouth was dry and his eyes throbbed. He had considered that maybe the radiation was getting through the suit and frying his brain. Maybe the slow march to madness was just acute radiation poisoning. Hell, maybe he had never woken up from being knocked out when they were inside the first chamber.

His mind continued to race; he kept working out alternate possibilities that could explain the unreality he found himself grappling with. Next, he mulled over the possibility that he was dead. Maybe he had died sometime shortly after entering the ship and this was, in fact, hell. God knew he probably deserved it, some of the stuff he had done. He felt he probably did. If he was dead and this was hell, then why was Crystal here? He knew little about her, but she didn't seem like she'd been a candidate for spending eternity burning with him.

The voice whispered again, breaking his train of thought, "You can be wherever you want to be, Kurt, but you're not dead yet. You will be soon, unless you kill her."

He shook his head, hoping Crystal wouldn't notice, and slogged on.

A few minutes later, the pair found themselves standing at a fork in the path. This new challenge brought Kurt's mental tug of war to a brief halt as Crystal asked, "What do you think, right or left?"

Kurt studied the diverging pathways. Other than the separation, both ways seemed equally terrible. The echoing moans and growls seemed to come from both sides. Kurt responded, "I know you're not going to like this, but I think we should each take one side, scout it out for a few minutes, then meet back here and decide."

"Yeah, sounds pretty stupid. I mean, splitting up for any amount of time in this fun house," Crystal quickly quipped.

Kurt, visibly frustrated, pushed back. "Just for a few minutes, see if either of us see anything hopeful. I want to get out of this place asap and don't want to waste hours going down the wrong path if we could have avoided it in the first place."

"That's easy for you to say; you're the one with the gun. I don't feel like being eaten alive by some old man snake."

Kurt pulled a handgun from inside his suit and held it out to Crystal. "Here, take this if it makes you feel better. Do you know how to use it?"

"It doesn't make me feel better. I don't think we should split up at all. And yes, I know how to use a handgun, Kurt."

Kurt, not waiting for a response, started down the left corridor. "I'll take the left; you take the right. We both walk five minutes in, turn around, meet back here. It's only ten minutes. Relax."

"Son of a bitch," Crystal muttered as she

reluctantly accepted the handgun. The cold metal felt foreign, and the dimly lit corridors seemed to stretch endlessly. As Kurt's figure disappeared down the left path, the shadows played tricks on the walls. Crystal, now alone, felt her breaths quickening, her muscles spasming all in protest at her mounting anxiety. She hesitantly began down the right path.

She hadn't realized the comfort that Kurt had brought her during their trek to this point. But now, alone in the corridor, the ominous sounds and shadows seemed heightened. Her steps were tentative now, attuned to any change in the tempo or pitch of the disconcerting sounds. She was also more aware of the glowing eyes that seemed to wink in and out of existence in her peripheral vision.

Crystal was looking down at her watch, realizing that she had walked less than a minute, when a gunshot rang out. "Kurt!" She screamed, turning on heel to sprint the way she had come. As she neared the exit of the corridor to the common junction, she slid on the rocky floor to a stop. Just before the opening to the common path, blocking her way out, was an amorphous black figure. Within its confines, silver shimmers rolled and glinted before fading away into its obsidian depths. Harsh whispers drifted to her from the direction of the mass. She thought that maybe the shadow was another trick of the ship, designed to keep her from assisting Kurt. Anger boiled in her as she thought of all she had been through, the loss of her coworkers, friends. Now this thing was trying to keep her from helping the one remaining person who had dared to explore the ship. She rushed into the shadow, hoping to go right through the optical illusion and reach Kurt. As she entered the smoke-like haze, the many whispers intensified. She felt strong, cold arms embrace her, and then her world went black.

CHAPTER TWENTY-FOUR

The crimson glow of the lightning transformed the woods into a scene bathed in blood. Ken scanned the tree line as he moved across the deserted back road. The mysterious shapes of the new horrific cohabitants lurked in the shadows of the forest. He still saw the flicker of glowing eyes moving from tree to tree. Ken thought that out in the countryside there would be no signs of the giant creatures he had brushed by in the city, but his recent run in at the creek reminded him they were everywhere.

He expeditiously passed a large pathway in the woods that he knew had not previously been there. Broken trees, some strewn into the roadway, marked the trail of some giant that recently crossed the street. To the opposite side of the roadway, Ken observed the passage went as far as he could see before being swallowed by the darkness.

A jolt ran through him as he thought of

the path's insidious creator. He was less than five miles from home; he sent a silent prayer that the monster hadn't stopped by there in his absence. Breaking from his thoughts, Ken looked at the gauge panel of the Bearcat and noticed he was dangerously low on fuel. He knew that if he could make it home, there were a few filled gas cans in the shed that could get him to a gas station. He shuddered at the thought of stopping at another gas station after the last incident.

Ken and Loki were a mile from the house when the Bearcat shuttered. "Cmon, you son of a bitch, not now!" Ken yelled. He stepped on the gas, giving it a momentary boost forward before the engine shut off. Ken used the remaining momentum to coast the vehicle a few hundred yards more before it rolled to a stop. "Looks like we're walking from here boy," he said to Loki. The dog's ears perked up at the sound of the 'W' word. He grabbed the shotgun and looped Loki's unattached leash around his waist, planning to keep it handy. With Loki having free roam, they exited the vehicle and Kurt said, "Close boy."

Attuning his senses to the world outside of the Bearcat, he noticed that the abnormal sounds of the foreign creatures seemed distant and faint now. The clearest sound being the hoot hoot hoo of a barn owl perched somewhere among the nearby branches. An absence of noises did little to quell the feeling of being exposed outside the shelter of the vehicle. The walk to his house was cold, their breath creating gigantic clouds of vapor that trailed them as they walked on. Ken's body tensed at every snap of a branch or rustle of leaves that came from the woods, ready to confront whatever might try to stop them from making it home. As he and Loki approached the start of the gravel driveway, the woods seemed to fall silent, the only sound the crunching of the gravel underfoot.

The woods lining the long driveway were shrouded in shadow, occasionally eerily illuminated by the lightning. A few minutes later, the house came into view, seemingly undisturbed from afar. As they approached the front door, the hairs on the back of Ken's neck stood. The front door, which had initially appeared closed, was slightly ajar. Looking at Loki, Ken said, "Find boy." He pushed the door open while raising the shotgun. Ken said in a low voice, "Sarah, Sarah, where are you?"

Ken and Loki descended the stairs in the entry of the bi-level house, Loki led the way with Ken close behind. Room by room, they cleared the downstairs, Ken calling out his wife's name in what was increasingly becoming a desperate search. As they moved up the steps to clear the upper floor, Ken noticed a few dark spots on the landing. His mind raced, considering all the worst-case scenarios. Ken pointed to the right, signaling for Loki to check the hallway while Ken went left.

Loki padded down the hallway to the bedrooms and almost immediately caught a whiff of the new, unpleasant odor. He hunched down, making himself low to the ground as he approached the bedroom of his humans. The door was wide open, and the scent grew stronger, mixed with the familiar smell of blood. Moving inside, Loki saw a figure hunched at the foot of the bed, making slurping sounds over a lump on the floor. Loki coiled his body in preparation and leaped at the creature.

Meanwhile, Ken was finishing clearing the kitchen when he heard a muffled snarl, immediately knowing that Loki had found something. He ran down the hall, his boots thumping on the hardwood floor. Entering the bedroom, he saw Loki latched onto the back of the leg of a horrendous biped creature. The gray-skinned thing lashed behind itself with sharp claws in an attempt to reach the snarling dog. Hearing Ken's entrance, the abomination spun to face him. The creature had no eyes, ears, or nose, just a small hole of a mouth lined with small needle-like teeth. It hissed at Ken, who raised the 12-gauge, and put a round into the creature's chest. Without waiting to see the result, he racked a fresh shell and put another shot into its head, painting the wall with bits of gore as the creature went limp, dropping to the floor.

Ken rushed to Loki, who was backing away from the collapsed body. He ran his hands over his partner, feeling for any injuries. After determining Loki was unharmed, he stood up and took an inventory of the bedroom. His heart caught in his throat as he saw the lump of flesh at the foot of the bed, barely discernible as human remains. His eyes welled with tears, he again internally admonished himself for all the decisions that had led to this. As he dropped to his knees, softly sobbing, Loki approached slowly, sensing his partner's despair.

Ken absorbed the wreckage of the room, catching sight of a lone man's shoe near the chaotic scene. He scanned further, noting the open, rummaged through closet, suggesting a hasty exit. Leaping to his feet, he dashed to the back sliding glass door, peering out at the vacant space where their vehicles usually rested. A surge of relief washed over him; his truck was absent from its usual spot. Sarah, he thought, must have loaded up Grant and made a swift escape.

Returning to the disheveled bedroom, Ken rummaged through the jeans attached to the mangled corpse, discovering a wallet. As he sifted through its contents, he unveiled an ID: Tim Goodson. Tim had been Ken and Sarah's friendly neighbor, an elderly man who graciously introduced himself upon their arrival, offering his tools for borrowing. Ken had shared anecdotes of his job with Tim during occasional visits. A twinge of guilt crept in as Ken realized he felt relief that it was Tim and not his own family.

Tim, a kind soul, likely came to check on Sarah and Grant when the ominous bang echoed through the air, followed by the encroaching darkness. Sarah had probably left already, and Tim, upon seeing the open door, fell victim to the monstrous entity Ken had just dispatched. Yet, a crucial question lingered: if Sarah had managed to escape, where had she gone, and what were her odds of survival in this surreal nightmare?

Ken tore through the house, anxiously searching for any clue about Sarah's whereabouts. The worry ate at him as he imagined the horrific possibilities. The idea that she could have headed to his city station briefly crossed his mind, but he quickly dismissed it, knowing Sarah was too smart for such a risky move.

Their bedroom yielded a minor relief; the missing suitcase suggested she had likely escaped unharmed. Frustration bubbled up as the search turned up nothing concrete about her location. Then, like a sudden revelation, Ken scolded himself mentally—how could he forget the fridge?

In the chaos of their opposite schedules, Ken and Sarah had relied on leaving notes for each other on the fridge—a makeshift communication hub. Rushing to the kitchen, Ken scanned the surface. A hastily written note, with Sarah's usually neat handwriting now jagged, caught his eye. The message was concise—Jack's cabin.

Another oversight brought in by exhaustion and nonstop adrenaline, Jack's cabin, of course. They had spent a week each summer at Sarah's brother's cabin every year since they had started dating. When the crap hit the fan, it would be an obvious choice for Sarah, far away from any major population centers. It was a brilliant choice to escape any man-made disaster. Ken felt a wave of pride for his quick-thinking partner before a terrifying thought quickly replaced it. Jack's cabin was six hours northwest of his current location. He lived less than an hour from the city and it had taken him an eternity to reach home. He hoped that his theory of the creatures being less numerous in sparsely populated areas held true.

Ken knew Jack had probably headed to the cabin as soon as he noticed the stars had disappeared. He had always gotten along with Sarah's brother, but the guy was a conspiracy theory survivalist type, Ken had always thought was a little nuts. In this particular scenario, he was thankful that the man was a little unhinged. The one time you're happy to be the friend of a doomsday prepper is when it's actually doomsday. If Sarah could make the journey there, he knew they would be well supplied and armed for most of the freaks he had run across in the past 28 hours.

A sense of urgency to catch up to Sarah and Grant motivated Ken to expeditiously load the leftover car with supplies. While running the provisions to the car, he internally debated taking the car straight to the cabin or going back for the Bearcat. The car could travel at a much faster clip than the armored vehicle, but the added protection of the Bearcat was invaluable. As he glanced at the ever-increasing red flashes in the sky, the uncertainty of when this nightmare would end helped him to reach a decision.

After making a quick trip to the shed for the gas cans, he and Loki peeled out of the driveway, spitting up loose gravel, turning out of the lane toward the Bearcat. Once at the Bearcat, Ken emptied the gas tanks into the rolling fortress, with Loki watching his back. He again thought about Sarah and Grant. The road to the cabin would be a long one on a normal day, and he hoped if he could not catch up to them that Sarah's wit continued to serve her well in this new reality. He thought about the horrors he had encountered and what new ones might await them. He felt a sense of hopelessness that was partially extinguished when the next flash of heat lightning showed the silhouette of the dog standing beside him.

CHAPTER TWENTY-FIVE

Aberdeen Maryland

A dozen mounted spotlights illuminated the craft in the dark lab. The smell of ozone intermingled with the metallic smell of blood lingering in the air. As Army Colonel Briggs looked over the blood-stained computer monitors of the command station, he spoke to the sergeant who had checked on the labyrinth after the world went dark.

"So, you think this is the source of the event? Where is everyone?"

"We don't know sir, we know the craft was emitting high levels of all types of energy and we know three scientists went in with one of ours, and there should have been a scientist and soldier out here monitoring them. Last footage we have is of the group entering the ship, right before everything went out."

"They went in, the ship. Where?" The Colonel asked, looking quizzically at the solid gray orb.

"They reported there was a doorway, sir. On the monitors, it looked like they had just walked through the side of the ship. I'm not sure, but I don't think they're making it back out."

"Once we make sure the base is secure from whatever the hell those things are, gather up some men and the remaining scientists and get them down here, sergeant."

EPILOGUE

Days of the horrific onslaught of darkness had passed by before someone at the base had thought of the potential connection between the monstrosities and the secret project. Because of the outage of most modern communication methods and the relentless battle with spectral man-eaters, the message from the project's head commander in DC hadn't reached the base until then. A small, battered convoy arrived at the proving ground with a message from DC, suggesting that the events unfolding in the world may be related to the secret project below. That was when the sergeant checked into the lab.

Crystal and the others, dealing with their own calamity within the ship, couldn't have known that the moment they moved the book from the podium, a chain of terrifying events had unfolded on the outside.

Within the first day of darkness, estimates surmised it had wiped out approximately one fifth of the human population. Communications trickled into the United States from Mexico and Canada, whose reports looked even more grim.

The United States, with its prolific reputation for being hard to conquer, its citizens being highly armed, had a fighting chance. This information wasn't available to Kara and Jeff, but their circumstances were not unique.

A scant few had traversed the distance that Ken had and survived the journey. The rest of the world was dark and because conventional communications were down, the United States could only assume other countries were dealing with the same. The oceans, formerly treacherous on their own, were now a death sentence to anyone attempting to navigate them.

Rumors had stirred, creatures swallowing ships whole and the US Navy's fleet had remained in their ports. Speculations swirled around the source of the darkness and the creatures within. The mysterious orb was now believed to be the epicenter of the event, but to what extent no one knew. The prevailing theory was an extraterrestrial invasion, only because the masses could not wrap their minds around the multiple planes of existence theory.

They deployed active-duty military personnel that were stateside in an attempt to take back parts of the country from the creatures. Reservists who could be reached were also called upon, but the fighting was a massive game of whack a mole. Without knowing how the abominations were getting here, the progress was slow. The creatures seemed to materialize out of nowhere and the government knew that until they discovered the access point, their impact would be minimal.

The power grid was mostly offline from what they thought was an electromagnetic field burst, and all attempts at bringing it back online had failed. Mobile networks were all offline, puzzlingly, landlines worked sporadically. The world was embroiled in a battle with the darkness and knew little of its adversary. The leaders of the U.S. now believed that the mysteries of the orb may hold the key to understanding the chaos.

Amid the upheaval of humankind, one thing was certain: it would entrench the survivors in a horrifying fight for survival for the foreseeable future.

PREVIEW OF BOOK TWO

The road ahead was a long one. Ken knew that the drive, normally six hours, would take him days. The limited visibility from the blackout darkness made moving slow. The obstacles in the form of unearthly abominations trying to eat him made it even slower. If he had known exactly when Sarah had fled their home, he wouldn't be in such a rush to reach the cabin. If she had left shortly after the bang, then he knew the only way he would catch up to her would be if something terrible had happened to her. He shuddered at the possibility of her encountering one of the beasts. His mind kept toying with him and suggesting that he had just missed her and needed to hurry. He knew this was probably not the case but he couldn't shake the feeling.

Ken and Loki were not far into their new quest before Ken's eyelids became heavy. He found them slowly closing on several occasions before being startled awake by the rumble strips on the scenic road. He had lost track of time during the nonstop terror ride and couldn't recall when he had last slept. Ken knew that there was only so long the human body could rely on adrenaline to stay awake. The thought of trying to sleep anywhere in this new world sent a shiver down his spine. Still, he searched the blackened, tree covered roadside for a resting spot.

There was a time not long ago when Ken had repeatedly pulled all-nighters for the job. Being forced to work overtime and granted only a two hour break to return home before the morning shift, he never attempted to sleep. That was many years ago, and only for one day straight, tops. He estimated he'd been awake for over two days now, though without a moon or sun, it was hard to be sure adrenaline could fuel a man only for so long and when the dump came, it hit hard.

He knew that he needed to find a suitable spot soon before his body shut down on him. The plan was to sleep inside the bearcat for a few hours before hitting the road again. Despite the armored exterior Ken was still apprehensive to stay in one spot for too long, some of the giant creatures he had seen would easily pick up the vehicle or swallow it whole.

Suddenly a deer sprinted across the road in front of the vehicle causing Ken to slam on the brakes. Wild eyed, and frothing at the mouth the animal looked exhausted, its ribs heaving and its nose expelling large clouds in the cold air. In close pursuit, a hairless four-legged monstrosity darted out from the woods. The creature had no resemblance to any earthly creature but Ken thought, hellhound, to himself. As the creature crossed the path of the road Ken gunned the throttle, clipping the rear end of the monster and sending it careening to the ditch on the side of the road. After landing there the abomination lay motionless.

Satisfaction crossed his face as he thought he may have saved one of God's remaining creatures on the hellscape that earth had become.

The brief encounter had momentarily revitalized Ken, but he recognized the pressing need for rest. The burning fatigue in his eyes warned him that if he didn't halt soon, he'd fall asleep at the wheel. Ken pressed on through the desolate rural landscape, weariness competing with his determination. Once-familiar farmland hinted at tales of a world now overrun by monsters. The relentless journey had worn him down; exhaustion tugged at his senses as he considered the decision of seeking refuge or chasing after Sarah.

AUTHORS NOTE

My sincerest thank you for lending me one of life's most precious resources, your time. Thank you for taking a chance to read a fellow horror novel enthusiast's work. I hope that I made it an exciting experience.

If you enjoyed this story, you could help me by leaving an honest review and continuing on in the series. Book two, The Keepers of Darkness is now available and there will be more to follow. You would also do me a great service by recommending this book to your friends and family that enjoy the genre. If you would like to reach out to chat, give recommendations, follow along for upcoming releases, or just to say hello you can find me at.

Instagram: thed.r.kane

Made in United States
Troutdale, OR
12/22/2024

27018279R00137